"Innocent? Tell Me What Happened In This Room?"

Cody demanded, his eyes dark and dangerous. "Or have you forgotten?"

Margaret remembered well the passion they hadn't saved for their wedding night. The wedding night that never came. "I haven't forgotten how nice you were to me then, how considerate, how generous, how, how…" She bit her lip. *She would not cry.* "You've changed, Cody. You've made it very clear how much you despise me now."

The taut lines around his mouth softened imperceptibly. "I don't despise you," he said gruffly. He traced a line around the curve of her cheek with one finger.

She drew a shaky breath. If he started being kind and sweet again, she'd have no defense against him. She'd be putty in his arms again.

Then Cody did the unthinkable.

He claimed her with a kiss. A kiss hotter than any kiss they'd shared before.

Dear Reader,

Hello! For the past few months I'm sure you've noticed the new (but probably familiar) name at the bottom of this letter. I was previously the senior editor of the Silhouette Romance line, and now, as senior editor of Silhouette Desire, I'm thrilled to bring you six sensuous, deeply emotional Silhouette Desire novels every month by some of the bestselling—and most beloved—authors in the genre.

January begins with *The Cowboy Steals a Lady,* January's MAN OF THE MONTH title and the latest book in bestselling author Anne McAllister's CODE OF THE WEST series. You should see the look on Shane Nichols's handsome face when he realizes he's stolen the wrong woman...especially when she doesn't mind being stolen or trapped with Mr. January one bit....

Wife for a Night by Carol Grace is a sexy tale of a woman who'd been too young for her handsome groom-to-be years ago, but is all grown up now.... And in Raye Morgan's *The Hand-Picked Bride,* what's a man to do when he craves the lady he'd hand-picked to be his brother's bride?

Plus, we have *Tall, Dark and Temporary* by Susan Connell, the latest in THE GIRLS MOST LIKELY TO... miniseries; *The Love Twin* by ultrasensuous writer Patty Salier; and Judith McWilliams's *The Boss, the Beauty and the Bargain.* All as irresistible as they sound!

I hope you enjoy January's selections, and here's to a very happy New Year (with promises of many more Silhouette Desire novels you won't want to miss)!

Regards,

Melissa Senate

Melissa Senate
Senior Editor

Please address questions and book requests to:
Silhouette Reader Service
U.S.: 3010 Walden Ave., P.O. Box 1325, Buffalo, NY 14269
Canadian: P.O. Box 609, Fort Erie, Ont. L2A 5X3

CAROL GRACE
WIFE FOR A NIGHT

SILHOUETTE *Desire*®
Published by Silhouette Books
America's Publisher of Contemporary Romance

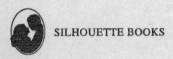

SILHOUETTE BOOKS

ISBN 0-373-76118-X

WIFE FOR A NIGHT

This edition published by arrangement with Harlequin Books S.A.

® and TM are trademarks of Harlequin Books S.A., used under license.
Trademarks indicated with ® are registered in the United States Patent
and Trademark Office, the Canadian Trade Marks Office and in other
countries.

Printed in U.S.A.

CAROL GRACE

has always been interested in travel and living abroad. She spent her junior year in college in France and toured the world working on the hospital ship *Hope*. She and her husband spent the first year and a half of their marriage in Iran, where they both taught English. Then, with their toddler daughter, they lived in Algeria for two years.

Carol says that writing is another way of making her life exciting. Her office is her mountaintop home, which overlooks the Pacific Ocean and which she shares with her inventor husband, their daughter, who is now twenty-one years old and a senior in college, and their seventeen-year-old son.

Prologue

The bus stopped in Second Chance, Wyoming, in a driving rain. One passenger got on. Her long white satin dress was plastered to her body, and she was breathing hard from her run through the streets. She sank into the first available seat, her heart pounding.

"Where to, lady?" the driver asked nonchalantly, as if he picked up runaway brides every day.

"Uh...Chicago."

"I go as far as Cheyenne," he said over his shoulder. "You can transfer there."

She nodded. *Please go,* she begged silently, staring straight ahead while the water dripped off her forehead and ran down her face. *Please leave before I lose my nerve. Before I get off and run back to the church. Before I make a mistake I'll regret the rest of my life.*

In answer to her plea, a muffled roar slowly rose in pitch as the bus lurched forward. The windows rattled but she didn't look right or left until they left Main Street. And then she wished she hadn't.

He was standing on the side of the road, the water running off his wide-brimmed hat, staring at her. His mouth set in a tight line. Their eyes locked, and her heart stopped beating. She couldn't think, she couldn't breathe.

His gaze drilled holes through her. She knew what he was thinking. How could she do it? How could she leave after last night? The most incredible night of their lives. The first time they'd made love. The first and last.

Her stomach quivered as she remembered his kisses burning a path down her body. His hand caressing the sensitive skin between her thighs. His tongue teasing, tantalizing, lingering. Branding her with his touch and his lips to make her his forever.

How could she walk out on him?

She couldn't. She jumped to her feet and yanked on the emergency cord. Nothing happened.

She opened her mouth to scream for the driver to stop, but no sound came from her throat.

Her knees buckled and she collapsed into her seat.

Margaret gripped the cold metal of the handrail in front of her with shaking hands. It was too late, too late to change her mind. Again. The bus lumbered on toward the highway and left him standing there, a tall man in a tuxedo, drenched to the skin and totally unaware of it.

Totally unaware of why she'd left him at the altar. Even though she'd tried to explain. Tried to tell him how she felt torn in two. Scared to stay and scared to leave.

But he'd refused to listen. Said it was prewedding jitters. Said everybody had them. But everybody wasn't nineteen years old. Everybody didn't have an aunt who told her she was too young to tie herself down. That she had a brilliant future ahead of her. If she left.

Margaret knew if she didn't leave now, she'd never leave. And if she never left, she'd never know if she could make it in the real world. The world outside this valley. For Cody, the valley *was* the world. All, the world he'd ever want. As long as he had her to share it with him.

And so he'd kissed away her fears. Dissolved her jitters with the slow-burning flame of passion. Silenced the voice inside her head that told her to take a chance, to find out who she was, now while she was still young and free.

Tears mingled with raindrops and caught in her eyelashes. The town faded from sight. And Cody was just a blur.

"I'm sorry," she whispered, pressing her forehead to the window, as the tears poured down her face. "So sorry."

He didn't hear her. And if he had, he wouldn't have believed her. He didn't understand her cold feet. But he was six years older. He knew exactly who he was and what he wanted. He didn't feel the lure of the unknown. Didn't dream of being somebody else, somewhere else. Where nobody knew your name or anything about you.

And he hadn't noticed the worn, weather-beaten faces of the guests as they watched her come down the aisle.

He didn't hear the words of her aunt echoing in her brain.... *You're only nineteen.... You're too young.... You've got your whole life ahead of you.... If he loves you he'll wait.... Margaret Kidder, you've got too much talent to spend your life plucking chickens for Sunday dinner....*

So at the last minute she'd turned and run out of the church. She was still running. Running to Chicago and art school, where she'd been offered a scholarship she'd be crazy to turn down. To a brilliant career. And if it didn't work out, Second Chance would always be there. But would he?

One

Six years later

Cody Ralston stood on the raised boardwalk in front of the old historic building and kicked the mud off his boots. The morning sun glittered on the window and bounced off the sign that said *Lonesome Cowboy,* The Magazine That Makes Dreams Come True. He gave a derisive snort before he knocked loudly and then walked in.

He ducked to avoid being speared by the pair of sun-bleached antlers hanging on the wall and crashed into her. She stumbled and almost fell. He caught her wrists in a viselike grip.

"You! What the hell are you doing here?" he demanded. Crazy. He must be nuts to come in here today. He should have known she'd be there. But there are some things that can't wait.

Margaret jerked out of his grasp as if she'd touched a

live electric wire. Then she gasped for breath. She wasn't ready for this. The way he towered over her, his eyes glittering dangerously, his fury just barely contained. With his broad shoulders in a worn leather jacket, his muscled thighs in faded denims, he exuded strength and raw masculinity.

"I'm here for the funeral," she said.

"Great," he seethed. "Skip the wedding and come for the funeral."

The color drained from her face. "I understand how you feel," she said, "but I was hoping…"

"Me, too. I was hoping I'd never see you again."

She winced as if he'd slapped her. "I was hoping we could be friends," she said, running her palms down her skirt.

"Not a chance," he said. "I've got all the friends I can use. But I'll let you know if there's an opening. Leave your name and number. But don't call me, I'll call you."

He watched her lick her lower lip. A nervous habit. And the memories came rushing back. Her lips meeting his, hot and eager. Their tongues joining in a wet and wild dance. Just looking at her made him ache with longing. And looking was all he was going to do. Even if she begged him. *Yeah, right.*

She shifted her weight from one high-heeled shoe to the other. "You have every right to be angry."

"Angry? Why would I be angry? I can't even remember why you left. Or when."

"Six years ago," she said. "And three months, seventeen days," she added under her breath.

If he didn't know better, he'd have almost thought she'd been counting. And that she'd thought about him as he'd thought about her, every one of those days. But he *did* know better. Word had filtered back by way of her aunt how Margaret was the toast of the town, a big success, both socially and professionally. "That long," he said as if the day and the date weren't engraved permanently in his mind. "Time flies when you're having fun."

"Are you?" she asked so poignantly, old buried feelings slammed into him like a barn door and knocked the breath out of him.

"Damn right. Just about as much fun as I can handle. But enough about me." He stuffed his hands in his pockets and looked at her through narrowed eyes. "Let's talk about you." Wait a minute. He didn't want to hear about her. Or her new life. He could imagine what it was like. The parties, the friends. He didn't need to hear any details. He didn't need any more pain than he'd already suffered. "What do *you* think about me?" he asked with a sardonic grin.

He felt her gaze travel the length of his body. Thank God he'd taken the time to clean his boots and give himself a haircut. Not that she cared. But he had his pride. For what it was worth.

"You've changed," she said at last, feeling the chill from his ice-cold blue eyes.

"No, *you've* changed."

"I owe you an apology," she said. If it was possible to apologize for what she'd done. Maybe she could explain, if he'd let her. Explain how it felt to be nineteen, confused and full of fears and frustrations. Maybe this time he'd understand. If he did, it would be worth the agony of having him lash out at her like this.

"You owe me more than that," he snapped.

"What can I do?" she said, digging her fingernails into her palms. Throw herself on the floor and beg for mercy? That wouldn't do any good. He'd probably just step over her on his way out the door. All these years she'd thought about him. Thought about meeting him again one day. Planning what to say. Having a chance to make things right. That day was here. But it wasn't going the way she'd planned. Things couldn't have been worse.

"You can get out of town. Get out and stay out."

She staggered backward, stung by the force of his words, until she bumped against the edge of the old oak desk. "I will," she said bravely. "Just as soon as I straighten out the magazine and arrange the funeral."

Margaret could have sworn he was going to stomp out, but he tossed his hat in the direction of the antler hat rack and took a seat in the straight-backed chair that faced the desk. So he wasn't through with her yet.

"Sorry about your aunt," he said.

She rubbed her wrists where she still felt the sting of his grip. She heard no sympathy in his voice. Only anger, just barely suppressed. She saw it in the taut muscles of his broad shoulders, and in the lines etched in his forehead. Was this the same man who'd once massaged her back to ease her cramps, who'd taken the abstract pictures she'd painted and proudly hung them all in his living room? She knew he was angry, but she'd hoped that in six years he might have forgiven her, maybe even mellowed. But no.

"I should have come sooner," she said, swallowing hard over the lump in her throat.

"Why didn't you? Afraid of what you'd find? That no one remembers you? No one in town gives a damn about you anymore?"

The cruel words cut to the bone. She gripped the edge of the desk and stared at the toes of her leather shoes without seeing them. Then she took a deep breath. "After all these years, after all we'd meant to each other, I thought…"

"You thought I'd be waiting with open arms? Not a chance!"

Her head snapped up and she felt his eyes bore into hers. The memories came flooding back with a vengeance. Their last night together. His arms open and waiting while she tore off her clothes in a fevered rush. His throbbing sexuality threatening to burst the buttons on his jeans. His eyes, then his mouth, devouring her aching, upturned breasts.

She could still feel the tingling of her own arousal as if it were yesterday. But it was six years ago, the night they broke their promise to each other and made love before marriage. The night he made her forget her doubts and fears. Twenty-four hours before the ceremony. The ceremony that never took place. And in six years she'd never found anyone else who'd tempted her to throw off her inhibitions or her clothes. She'd buried herself in her work. And for what? She hadn't succeeded as she'd imagined and she'd lost the only man she ever loved.

She crossed her arms over her chest, hoping he hadn't noticed her nipples tighten and pucker under his bold gaze that raked her up and down. But the knowing look on his face told her he had. Her face flushed.

"I didn't know how serious the situation was," she said. "Or I would have come."

She walked around the edge of the desk to sit in her aunt's swivel chair to put some space between them. Despite the mud-spattered boots, the dark brown hair looking like it had been cut with a pair of sheep shears, he was still the sexiest man she'd ever seen.

With his blatant masculinity, he made all other men look like cardboard cutouts. And he still had the power to make the flow of desire run through her veins, thick and hot and heavy. She didn't trust herself anywhere within spitting distance of him.

"What can I do for you?" she asked coolly, aware that he was still staring at her. Making her skin feel shivery cold while she was burning hot on the inside. "How about taking an ad in next month's *Lonesome Cowboy?* We're running a special."

"An ad in a lonely hearts magazine?" he asked incredulously. "Not me. I'm already married."

A sharp stab of disappointment hit her like a knife in the chest. Of course he was married. A man whose touch could set off fire alarms, whose searing blue gaze could turn a woman inside out. Did she imagine he was still carrying a torch for her? If so, he'd made it abundantly clear today that he wasn't.

"I'm—I'm happy for you," she stammered. "Ranch life can be lonely."

"Tell me about it," he said bitterly.

She *was* happy for him. And happy for herself. Because now she could return to Chicago knowing it was really over this time. Then why did it hurt like a branding iron to hear he was married, *to someone else?*

Learning that Cody was married had nothing to do with the empty hollow feeling in the pit of her stomach. If she was disappointed it was just that she wanted to sell an ad—to show Aunt Maud she could do it. Aunt Maud who, from some heavenly cloud, was probably watching every move she made. She could almost hear her now. *Margaret, don't let anyone get out without selling them an ad.*

"I'm here about something else. Someone else."

"Really. Who?"

"A friend."

The way she studied him made the old familiar anger rise in his throat and gag him. The gall of her to look at him as if she didn't believe him. As if she thought *he* would have to advertise to find a woman. Apparently she hadn't gotten wind of his well-earned reputation as the town stud these past six years. She'd believed him when he said he was married.

"My friend wants to run an ad," he said curtly. "It's fairly urgent or I wouldn't have come in. I would have waited." Waited until hell froze over, if it was up to him. But it wasn't. This was a favor he owed. Big time.

"Then let me tell you about the special. It's a 'run till

you sell' deal. We run the ad until you find a wife. For one flat fee. As long as it takes.''

''Not me. My friend,'' he insisted, pounding his fist on his thigh. He let his gaze roam from her glossy dark hair drawn back in a French braid to the swell of her breasts under her silk blouse.

Then he drew a ragged breath. She was no longer a beautiful girl. She was a beautiful woman. A shaft of desire shot through his body. Straight to the groin. As unwanted and unexpected as she was. The pounding of his own blood filled his ears.

Why did she have to come back? And why couldn't she be skin and bones and a hank of hair? Instead of lush curves and thick chestnut curls that once tumbled over her bare shoulders. Why, why, why? He was doing so well. He'd almost forgotten how her voice trembled when she was nervous, how one look from those soft doe eyes and he'd do anything for her. Anything. Not anymore, he vowed. Those days—the days he'd made a fool of himself over Margaret Kidder—were gone forever.

His jeans were painfully tight against his growing, aching arousal. He slouched down in his chair, trying to ignore his throbbing manhood, and reminded himself Margaret no longer belonged in this valley. By the look of her clothes and the elusive, expensive scent that floated his way, she'd outgrown him and the town.

''A friend,'' she repeated. ''Tell me about him.'' She attached a form to a clipboard, selected a sharpened pencil and looked at him. ''Occupation?''

''Cowboy.''

She had it written before he'd said the word. ''How did you know?'' he asked.

She looked up at him from under improbably long lashes. ''Just a lucky guess. I just remembered what they say about cowboys.''

"What, that their horse is their best friend and their spurs go jingle, jangle, jingle?"

She shook her head. "That they never cry and they're always polite to women."

"That's right. You could do worse, you know."

"Me?" Her faced flushed the color of a wild poppy. "I'm just as married as you are."

A cold chill of fear went up his spine. He looked at her ringless fingers still holding tight to her clipboard and held his breath. She couldn't be married. No, no, no.

"To my job," she explained.

A surge of relief almost swamped him. "Which is?" he asked.

"Can we get back to your friend and the ad?"

He shrugged. "Why not?"

"Age?"

"Let's say 'young at heart'?"

"Eyes?"

"Twenty-twenty."

She raised her head and looked into his eyes for a long moment. His heart thundered as he battled an urge to get a long hot taste of her mouth. A taste like red ripe berries. Dammit, why hadn't he waited till the magazine was sold and then placed the ad for Jake? If Jake weren't so totally bummed out, he was practically suicidal. Damn!

"I meant the color."

"Blue," he said shortly.

They continued, covering weight, one hundred and seventy-five pounds, and height, six foot three, and other important statistics; then she asked what kind of woman his friend was looking for.

Cody let his cynical gaze stray to the pictures on the wall of the happy couples united by the efforts of Ms. Maud "Muddy" Retton and *Lonesome Cowboy* magazine. The sappy smiles, the idiotic grins, the wedding dresses and the tuxedos all turned his stomach, reminding him of the bride who didn't make it down the aisle and a man left waiting at the altar. He wanted to grab her by the shoulders and trap her against the wall. Ask her if she'd suffered half as much as he did. If she'd ever paced the floor at night because she couldn't sleep. If she'd dreamed about him when she *did* sleep. If she'd ever regretted her decision for one minute. But deep down, he knew she hadn't. She'd walked out on him and never looked back.

"Someone different," he said, pinning her with his gaze. "But not too different," he cautioned. "Someone who'd fit in, who wouldn't mind the short winter days, being snowbound on occasion. Who doesn't shrink from hard work and who'd look forward to the long winter nights under the covers with her man. Someone who *likes* getting up at daybreak and making coffee and biscuits for her family. Building a future with a husband and kids..."

She stopped writing. Her knuckles were white. How dare he bring all this up? Insinuate she'd left because she was afraid of hard work and took the easy way out.

"We have a large subscribership," she said with stiff lips, "but it doesn't include any saints that I know of. Maybe your friend could lower his expectations just a touch. Did it ever occur to him that most women want something more than loneliness, isolation and round-the-clock labor?"

"Including you?" he asked, his blue eyes icy cold. "That's the reason you left, isn't it?"

"You know why I left. I told you how I felt, but you didn't listen. Then that night...the night..."

"Quit stuttering. I know what night you mean."

"I explained it all in the letter. The one you never answered," she said under her breath. She didn't tell him how long she'd waited for his answer. How it felt to reach into her mailbox day after day, month after month, and come up empty-handed. The disappointment, the despair was like a wound that wouldn't heal. How hard could it have been for him to send her a letter, just a note to say he was okay and that he forgave her?

"What was I supposed to say?" he demanded coldly. "That I understood? I didn't. I'll never understand how a woman can make love with a man one night and walk out on him the next day. Unless it didn't mean anything to her."

She set her clipboard on the desk, carefully, to hide her shaking hands. "Cody, what's the point of dredging up painful memories? The past is the past. I've got so much to do—the magazine, the funeral—and I'm sure you've got cows to feed and fences to mend, whatever..." She trailed off, unable to think with him looking at her like that.

After all this time he could still send a wave of sensual heat her way, weakening her defenses, making it hard to concentrate on anything but him. Reminding her of when she was nineteen and so madly in love, he filled her every waking thought. He'd been everything to her. His love had made her whole. After a lonely childhood with just an eccentric aunt for company, she'd had a family. She'd had Cody. That was then. Six years ago. This was now. Now she had nobody.

If only he'd kiss her. Just one kiss and get it over with. It would break the tension that filled the small overheated office. Convince her that she'd made the right decision after all. And then they could both get on with their lives.

She stared at him, willing him to leap across the desk and take her in his arms. Capture her lips in a possessive kiss. Invade her mouth with his tongue and massage, stroke and tease until she'd had enough. But he didn't. Of course not. He hated her. And she didn't blame him. If the situation had been reversed, if he'd left her at the altar, would she hate him?

She took a deep breath to stop the muscles from con-

stricting round her heart and blinked back a tear. She
couldn't hate him. No matter what he did to her. "Back
to the ad," she said groping for a copy of the latest issue
of *Lonesome Cowboy* at the edge of the desk. "Why don't
I read you one of our prize-winning ads, just to give you
an idea of what it takes to get a woman up here to brave
the blizzards and the loneliness…and the headless chickens." She gave Cody a brief glance over the top of the
glossy cover and opened it to a premarked page.

Cody stared off into space. Let her read, let her suggest,
let her write the whole damn ad if she wanted to. The
office no longer felt stuffy to him. It felt cool enough to
stimulate every nerve end, and the sound of her voice,
like warm honey, made him ache with awareness. And
the memories came flooding back. Of the time he'd had
the flu and she'd sat at his bedside, forcing endless cups
of tea and honey down his throat, her cool hands on his
fevered forehead. To this day he couldn't drink tea;
couldn't even smell it without remembering how much
he'd missed her. Every hour of every day. And how much
he'd loved her.

"'I'm tired of being alone,'" she read. "'I have a great
life in the great outdoors, fantastic friends and so much I
want to share with the right woman. Underneath a rough
exterior is a heart of gold and a romantic soul. Sponta-
neous, warm, loving, sincere, shy at times and yet confident, very successful.'" She paused and set the magazine
on the desk. She'd put him to sleep. He was so excited
to see her that he'd conked out in a hardwood chair. So
much for old times.

"Cody?"

"Who *is* this guy?" he demanded, opening his eyes
and straightening his spine. "Nobody I know."

"Probably not. But he was flooded with answers, as
Aunt Maud would tell you if she were here. As you can
see…" She held up the magazine to show him, grateful

to have something between them, even a color photograph of a barrel-chested man with a shy, yet confident smile. "He's just an ordinary guy. Women don't care about looks. Not like men. Women care about what's underneath."

He narrowed his eyes. "Where'd you hear that?"

"It's common knowledge. Shall we get back to your friend?"

Suddenly Cody was sick of talking to Margaret about his friend and marriage and the nonsense it took to find what passed for love. Love. He used to believe in love. A long time ago. He stood up. "Just write something like that guy did. And I'll bring in a picture."

She stood and walked around the desk to face him. And instantly wished she hadn't. He was too close, so close she could feel the heat rise off his body, making her pulse race and her knees wobble. The dark stubble that lined his cheekbones tempted her to trace the outline of his stubborn jaw with the pad of her thumb.

Her heart started to pound. The need to touch him, to feel him touching her grew stronger by the minute, and threatened to overwhelm her and make her do something she'd regret.

"Why can't your friend come in himself?" she asked when she'd finally caught her breath.

"Scared," he said briefly. "Embarrassed. It's not easy to put yourself on the block like this, laying all your secrets bare in some national magazine, admitting to the world you can't find somebody on your own."

"Is that what you think?" she asked, her eyes softening.

"It's what I know. Look at you," he instructed, jabbing his finger in her direction. His eyes clashed with hers. "You're feeling sorry for him. Well, he doesn't want your sympathy, and I don't blame him. All he wants is a wife.

Someone he can count on. To build a future with. To stand by him through thick and thin.''

"Everything I'm not. Is that it?"

"If the shoe fits…" he said.

He backed toward the door, and leaned against it, looking unbearably arrogant. As if he knew he had the power to reduce her to a quivering mass of jelly with just a look. "Don't forget to arrange for Ladies' Night at the Sundance Saloon," he said. "It was your aunt's project, you know."

"I *didn't* know. But I don't think…"

"Don't think? Well, you ought to. Think about your obligations to the town. To the people here. We may not live up to your high standards, but hell, our simple pleasures might amuse you."

"I didn't come back to be amused," she told him. "I came to bury Aunt Maud."

"I don't think she'd mind if you cracked a smile now and then."

Margaret's mouth almost turned up in a reluctant smile until she realized he was making fun of her. She clamped her lips together.

"Ladies' Night's a good place to scare up business, Muddy always said," he continued. "Every bachelor for miles around shows up."

"Be sure to tell your friend."

"Don't worry. He'll be there if I have to drag him by the collar," Cody said. "That is, if you won't stare at him or anything." *The way you're staring at me now.*

She couldn't help it. Couldn't help staring, at his leather jacket, at the wrinkled flannel shirt underneath it. Wondering if he'd come in just to see her today. Had he dreamed of her for six years as she'd dreamed of him? Had he replayed their conversations, relived their fights, their reconciliations, their sparring and their laughter? No, obviously he hadn't given her a thought. He'd only come to rub it in that he was married and she wasn't. There was an aching void in the area of her heart as she wondered who, where, when...and why her aunt hadn't told her.

She blinked and brought herself back to his friend's plight. "No, of course I won't stare. But I would like to meet him."

"I'll ask him," he said, "if he wants to meet you."

She shrugged as if it didn't matter and the sweater she had draped over her shoulders slid to the floor. Before she could move, he'd picked it up, and with one swift motion, tied it around her waist. His fingers burned a hole through the sweater and her blouse, his touch scorching its way right to her soul.

By tugging, he brought her closer to him. So close she could see the heat of passion in his dark blue eyes. Why didn't he kiss her? Because he didn't *want* to kiss her. He'd rather toy with her. Taunt her. Tempt her.

He reached behind him for the doorknob. "See ya around, then," he said and let himself out.

She leaned back against her aunt's spacious desk, wondering what ever possessed her to think she could run into Cody Ralston after six years, say hello and then goodbye. If all the customers were like this... But of course they weren't. There was nobody like Cody. If she'd fooled herself thinking there was, it had only taken a few minutes to remind her he was one of a kind.

Margaret glanced at the antlers-turned-hat-rack and let out a jagged sigh. He'd forgotten his hat. She lifted the Stetson from its perch, thinking how impossibly good-looking he was in it. Or out of it. With a quick glance out the window to make sure he was gone, she put it on her head, tilted it at a jaunty angle and let her mind wander.

How many times had she relived their last night together? Pictured his hat sailing across the room before he ripped his jeans off and stood there in all his throbbing naked splendor. The room spun around. The years fell away and she was nineteen again.

Young, eager, burning with passion, her eyes devouring every glorious inch of her aroused lover. Did his muscles still ripple? she wondered. Was his tan line still low on his hips? Did he still wear boxer shorts or none at all under his tight jeans? Just then the door swung open, the wind blew the papers off her desk and he appeared again in the doorway. Caught in the act, Margaret froze.

Cody stuffed his hands in his back pockets and stared, blatantly enjoying her discomfort. "Hand it over," he demanded. When she didn't obey immediately, he reached for his hat and, as he removed it from her head, his fingers grazed her cheek and roughly tangled in her hair. Her face, already flushed from shock and embarrassment, flamed from the heat of his touch.

"Funeral at two o'clock Thursday?" he said.

She nodded mutely. And then he was gone.

He was a busy man. Couldn't hang around teaching Margaret lessons in manners she sorely needed. Or in composure. She sure looked rattled when he'd caught her with his hat on.

But this was no time to think about Margaret and how she looked with or without his hat perched on her head. She was beautiful and she knew it. She probably had every man in Chicago at her feet. But this was not Chicago. In Second Chance, people had different standards. They looked for loyalty, devotion and faithfulness.

He could hear Aunt Maud now. *If that's what you're looking for, Cody, you need a dog, not a wife.*

He'd miss her and her astute comments. Everyone else would, too. Everyone was talking about her today, around the cracker barrel in the general store, but strangely enough, nobody mentioned the return of her niece. And neither did Cody. It wasn't that he'd forgotten about her.

The scent of her perfume followed him wherever he went. And the ache in his gut only got worse. How could she prance back into town as if nothing had happened? As if he had no feelings at all.

He had half a mind to go back in there and tell her he wasn't married after all. He'd tell her he could have any woman in town he wanted. It was just that he didn't want any of them.

But to go back to that office and watch her dusky nipples strain the fabric of her blouse, and *not* lower his head to nuzzle her breasts? To gaze at her long legs and not imagine them wrapped around his waist? Not a chance.

The next time he ran into her would be at the funeral. And after that, there would be no next time. He'd never have to see her again. That would be a relief. Sure it would.

Somehow Margaret managed to get through the rest of the day without accomplishing anything but sitting at her desk, staring off into space and losing herself in daydreams about the cowboy she'd deserted.

If he weren't already married, she would have suggested a decent haircut and an ironed shirt. He was still so...untamed, so...rugged, so...virile... She gave an involuntary shiver. So...sexy.

She made a list of things to do.

1. Lay out May issue.
2. Pay bills.
3. Answer reader letters.
4. Get Cody out of mind.

But at six o'clock, as the sun was sinking behind the Granite Mountains, Margaret still hadn't accomplished any of them. Especially the last, number four. So she left the office, locked the door behind her and drove her aunt's bright red Bronco to her house.

Then she checked up on Babou, her aunt's beloved pet, sat down to a lonely dinner and wondered what Cody had been doing these past six years. Besides getting married. Her aunt had always been strangely silent on his activities. She never thought he was good enough for her niece. Then, when Margaret left, she couldn't do enough for him, as if she was trying to make up for their breakup. She'd wanted so badly for Margaret to have her chance to succeed wildly where Maud hadn't, in the big city.

Well, Margaret had had her chance and hadn't succeeded very well, either. That didn't mean she wouldn't give it another try. But before she left town, she'd help Cody's friend find a wife. Yes, she would.

It wouldn't make up for the grief she'd caused him. It wouldn't erase the guilt that tormented her every sleepless night. But it was something, something that seemed important to him. It might take some creative copywriting, an extra trip to the printer to squeeze his friend into the May issue, but it was the least she could do, she told herself as she gazed out into the vast, dark empty valley, after what she'd done to him.

Two

It was a beautiful funeral. Maud had left explicit instructions. White doves were released into the blue Wyoming sky as the casket was lowered into the ground. Margaret lifted her eyes to watch the birds disappear into the atmosphere as the Methodist minister gave a short eulogy. And before she knew it, the "celebration of life" moved on to the saloon, and with it, most of the populace of Second Chance who'd come to say goodbye to their most colorful character.

Wending her way alone out of the hillside cemetery, Margaret tripped over a small tombstone. She would have fallen if a strong hand hadn't grabbed her arm and jerked her up. His touch sent a jolt of current through her arm that shook her to the soles of her low-heeled black shoes.

"Cody," she gasped. It had to be him. No one else had the power to make her feel as if she'd been struck by lightning. She glanced up to see if he'd been likewise affected, but his expression was grave and solemn. After all, it was a cemetery, she reminded herself. Regaining her balance, she tried to pull her arm away, but his fingers tightened around the black silky fabric of her suit.

Once again his fingers set off a chain reaction she was helpless to ignore. The chills that raced across her skin, raising goose bumps. The heat that shimmied up her spine. Reminding her of what she'd missed all these years.

He dropped her arm. It was obvious he didn't feel a thing.

"I thought it went pretty well," she said to fill the awkward silence as they walked toward the road.

"For a funeral."

She snuck a glance at him. He looked at her. And looked away. But not before she saw something like white-hot anger blaze from his blue eyes. Anger in the middle of a graveyard. He despised her. Could hardly wait for her to leave.

Her aching heart beat out a warning. *Stay away from Cody Ralston. If you value your sanity. Take his advice and hit the road. Forget finding his friend a wife. The risk of falling for him again is too great. He's not the same. He's changed. And he's married, for heaven's sake.*

The idea of Cody tangled in the sheets of his king-size bed with someone else, his *wife,* made her vision blur. Involuntarily she gripped his arm.

Very deliberately he pried her fingers off as if her touch was repellent to him. "What next?" he asked, his voice as cold as a Wyoming winter freeze.

She swallowed her hurt pride over the lump in her throat.

"Next? The party at the saloon," she said. "Just the way she wanted it. Free drinks and free food and no tears." She gave him a sideways glance. "No problem for you, being a cowboy."

"And you?" he asked.

She opened her mouth to reply, but bleak despair settled over her like a black cloud. The death of her beloved aunt, the loss of Cody. The realization that she meant nothing to him, that he'd never missed her and hardly knew she'd been gone, finally sank in.

After putting up a brave front for the past three days, her throat clogged with tears. She drew a deep shaky breath, buried her head in her hands and sobbed uncontrollably.

Cody stiffened. A bucking bronco, a runaway stallion, a stampeding bull were nothing compared to Margaret's tears.

He knew what he had to do—get the hell out of there and join the others at the saloon before things got any worse. But he couldn't leave now, with her falling apart like this, so he put his hands on her shoulders. Big mistake. The next thing he knew her face was pressed against his chest, tears soaked through his shirt all the way to his skin. The scent of wild roses filled his senses.

With a groan of protest that came from deep within him, he pulled her tight against him and ran his hand soothingly over her back. He didn't want to be her friend or her anything else. He shouldn't be doing this. But right now, he couldn't let her out of his embrace.

Finally, she lifted her glistening eyes to him and took a deep, shuddering breath. "Shall we go?" she said, looking embarrassed.

"If you're through." The words were harsh, he realized, and cursed himself inwardly. Then he remembered that he had to keep his distance from her. And being Mr. Nice Guy wouldn't help matters.

"Oh, no." Margaret frowned as the hearse disappeared from view on the road below them. "There goes my ride. I'm afraid...I have to ask you for a lift to town."

He didn't answer. He didn't want her riding with him, but he couldn't say no. Silently, they walked to his truck parked at the edge of the road.

She got into the front seat with a boost from him, just a shove upward on her bottom, the black silky fabric cool beneath his touch. He slammed the door with more force than necessary. Once he was in the seat beside her, he watched as she buckled up, just as she'd always done. As if she'd never left. When *was* she leaving? They were halfway to town before he asked.

"How soon are you leaving?"

She stared straight ahead. "As soon as possible, believe me."

Cody shifted into third gear and the truck sputtered and stalled. Alarmed, Margaret shifted in her seat and her eyes swerved in the direction of the dashboard. He pushed the gas pedal to the floor and the truck leapt forward. He breathed a sigh of relief. This was not the time for a stall or a breakdown. Not with Margaret on board.

"Do you think I like it here?" Margaret asked. She waved a hand at the grazing land on either side of the road, at the wheat grass and the tufted fescues blowing in the wind. To him it was a beautiful sight. To her, obviously not. Not anymore. "Do you think I'm not dying to leave?"

"I'm sure you are. I'm sure you can hardly wait to get back and do whatever it is you do. Whatever it is that's so much better than staying here."

"Do you really care?"

"Not much. I was making polite conversation, which is more than I can say for you. What *do* you do, work for the CIA?"

"I'm an interior designer. In Chicago. Is that polite enough for you?"

"Are you good at it?" he asked.

"I'm very good, but so are hundreds of other people. It's a competitive field."

"Like raising buffalo."

"It's not the same. People have to eat, but they don't have to hire a designer."

"They don't have to eat buffalo," he said.

"I didn't know you raised buffalo."

"Leaner meat, more protein, better for you."

"What does it taste like?" she asked, turning to look at him.

He met her gaze for a brief moment as they approached Main Street. "You can quit the polite stuff now," he said. "We're here." He pulled up in front of the Sundance Saloon.

Margaret felt like he'd slapped her in the face. He'd made it clear he didn't care about her, but she really did want to know about his life. Furious, she grabbed the door handle, jerked the door open and slid out of his truck before he'd come to a complete stop.

"Hey," he yelled, but she was crossing the boardwalk by then, edging her way through the crowd to slip into the bar.

The noise was deafening. The band she'd hired was blasting away in the corner. Laughter filled the air. That and cigarette smoke. She'd forgotten there was no anti-smoking ordinance in Second Chance. She circulated, giving everyone a chance to offer condolences.

"This is just what your aunt would have wanted," someone assured her.

"She had a great life, you know," someone else told her.

Margaret nodded.

"She used to say, 'Live every day as if it was your last.'"

If today *had* been her last, Aunt Maud would have

danced, laughed and smoked, and taken a lover to bed at the end of the evening.

She would not have avoided Cody Ralston as her niece was doing. It wasn't hard to do. There were so many people there. But Margaret was aware of his presence. Again and again her eyes were drawn to the tall figure with the brown hair falling over his forehead, a glass in his hand.

He'd removed his suit jacket and loosened his tie and was looking down at some blond woman in a low-cut red dress. The dress was totally inappropriate for a funeral. Even for one like this—a celebration of life. While Margaret watched, he tilted the woman's chin up and brushed her lips with his. A wave of nausea caught her. How could he, a *married* man.... Margaret turned her head and took a large gulp of the drink someone had handed her. Unless that was his wife.

The next time she saw him he was leaning against the bar with *another* woman, one who was laughing at something he'd said. She hated this woman in her tight black dress and her bright red hair and her loud laugh. Was *that* his wife?

Margaret took a deep breath and headed toward the bar, edging her way through the noisy mourners.

"Great party," someone said.

"Maud would have loved it."

By the time Margaret reached the bar, Cody's "friend" had disappeared, leaving Cody leaning against the bar with an empty glass clenched in his hand and an unfathomable look in his eyes.

"Enjoying yourself?" he asked.

"Yes, thank you," Margaret said.

Cody took a bottle from the bar and filled both his and Margaret's empty glasses. "So am I," he said.

"I noticed. Which one of those ladies was your wife?" she asked stiffly.

He drained his glass and poured another. "None of the above."

She rocked back on her heels. "Your behavior is despicable for a married man."

"Well, then, here's to the single life," he said, raising his glass to hers. "Isn't that what your aunt would have said?"

She sipped her drink, eyeing him warily over the rim of her glass. "She was married twice, you know."

"I forgot."

"You seem to have forgotten that you're married, too. When can I meet your wife?" Margaret asked.

"You can't."

"I suppose she's back at the ranch, baking biscuits."

"She would be."

"If she weren't polishing your boots, right?"

"Wrong. Nobody polishes my boots."

"No, they just lick them."

"Why, Margaret, what a sharp tongue you have in that sweet little mouth," he drawled, his gaze honing in on her lips.

She longed to come up with another barb, something that would pierce that know-it-all, arrogant armor he wore like a second skin, but all she could think of was his tongue plundering her mouth, her tongue mating with his, the strength of his arousal, his lips setting her on fire. What was wrong with her anyway?

When his eyes wandered and he winked at someone on the other side of the room, she turned and saw the object of his attention was a woman in a snug knit pants outfit.

"Is that your wife?" she demanded.

He shook his head.

Margaret's face flamed. "You're shameless. Flirting

with every woman in town. What kind of a wife would put up with this kind of behavior? I certainly wouldn't!''

His gaze swerved back to her. ''Good thing I didn't marry you, then.''

''Who *did* you marry?''

''Nobody.''

''What?''

''I never said I had a wife. I said I was married…to the ranch.''

''Oh.'' A surge of relief rushed through her, so strong, her knees shook and she reached for the edge of the bar to steady herself.

''And I haven't flirted with every woman in town,'' Cody said, setting his glass on the bar. ''Not yet.'' And he walked away.

The hours dragged by, during which she was tormented by watching Cody and his admirers. When the last mourner staggered out of the bar, Margaret wrote a check to cover the band and the drinks. With her head pounding, her eyes red and stinging, her body aching with longing for someone and something she couldn't have, she drove home to Maud's house and burst into tears for the second time that day.

But this time there was no one to wrap her in his strong arms, to make her forget the past and ignore the future.

She was stuck with her memories. Of being nineteen and racked with indecision. Her aunt telling her to go, Cody telling her to stay. As the wedding date approached, she'd felt the mountains that ringed the town close in on her. Cody had told her not to worry. Kissed away her fears. Burned them up in fires of passion. But the fears had come back. And followed her down the aisle of the church until she realized she couldn't go any farther. Then she'd turned and run.

Cody stepped into the kitchen of his low, rambling ranch house, stripped off his white shirt and tossed it over a chair. As he reached into the refrigerator for a beer, he almost didn't see his foreman at the table eating a bowl of cold cereal.

"Nice funeral?" Jake asked.

"Yeah, I guess so. If you like that kind of thing. Where were you?"

"Wasn't in the mood for a funeral. So I was workin' on the thresher."

He surveyed the old man with the weather-beaten face and the sad blue eyes and he was filled with compassion. The guy had given so much to the ranch and to Cody's family, he owed him a debt he could never repay. He took a seat at the table opposite his foreman and clasped Jake by the arm.

"I'll fix the thresher," Cody said. "It's the market for buffalo I can't fix. Animals just stand out there in the field eating up the profits. Staring at me. Daring me to sell them. Maybe I shouldn't have sunk so much capital into buffalo. One big order and I thought I was set. But as I was saying to Margaret, people don't have to eat buffalo. They can eat beef or lamb, and it looks like they are."

"As you was saying to who?" Jake asked, his eyes wide.

Cody clenched his hand around the beer can. "Margaret's back in town," he said.

"What for?"

"Good question."

"Gonna take over the magazine?"

"At least long enough to get your ad in there. I'll see to that."

"If it's too much trouble..."

"It's no trouble at all," Cody lied. For him, anything

to do with Margaret was more trouble than anyone deserved.

"She still pretty?" Jake asked.

"Who?" Cody asked, deliberately obtuse.

"You know who."

Cody shrugged. "I didn't notice." Didn't notice that her eyes were the color of maple syrup and her body just didn't quit.

"Not your type anyway."

"What is my type?"

Jake drew his bushy eyebrows together. "Somebody who'd fit in, who wouldn't mind the loneliness or the long winters…"

"Who'd bake biscuits at five in the morning and then feed the chickens," Cody continued.

"Sounds like a saint," Jake remarked.

Cody gave a rueful smile. "That's what she said." With heavy feet he walked down the hall to take a shower. He wasn't looking for a saint. He wasn't looking for anybody. Didn't he just spend the afternoon flirting with every good-looking woman in town? Every good-looking woman but one. And that was *her* problem, not his.

The lawyer's office was located above the dry-goods store in the same cluster of restored buildings as *Lonesome Cowboy*. Two days after the funeral, Margaret knocked on the door bearing the nameplate of Clifford Ross, Attorney at Law, stenciled in gold Gothic letters. After Clifford let her in to the cool dimly lighted office, she stifled a gasp of surprise to see Cody Ralston at the end of the table. What was *he* doing here? Who invited him?

"You know everyone here?" the attorney asked her.

She nodded, smiling politely at the faces around the table. When she got to Cody, she forgot about everyone else. He regarded her with a frosty look that caused her smile to fade, and her heart to thump wildly against her ribs.

Clifford cleared his throat and peered over his bifocals. "Mrs. Retton amended her will on the evening of her surgery and called me to her bedside to witness it," he explained.

Margaret felt a pang of guilt. She should have been there, not Clifford. She was family. Why hadn't her aunt called her? Margaret reached for her notepad and a pencil to take notes.

"'To my niece, Margaret, my only living relative, I leave all my worldly goods—except for my beloved pet, Babou, whom I suspect she doesn't really like—if she fulfills the following requirements. One—assuming control of the magazine I founded, *Lonesome Cowboy*. And two—living in my house for a minimum of one year, during which time she makes a concerted effort to find a husband to spend the rest of her days with, a goal that eluded me.'"

Margaret gasped, met Cody's gaze and looked away.

"'If the terms of the will have not been fulfilled, the bulk of my estate will revert to the National Wildlife Foundation.'"

Clifford paused. "Rather unusual, but then we are—I mean were—dealing with an unusual woman, if you don't mind my saying so, Miss Kidder."

"Not at all," Margaret said, her mind spinning. Running the magazine, finding a husband... The things her aunt never wanted for her. Why now, at the end of her life, had Aunt Maud decided that Margaret belonged in Second Chance instead of Chicago? Why running a magazine instead of the job she was doing? Why a husband when she'd always claimed a woman was better off pursuing a career than a man?

"Oh, and there's something else. A request tied to a stipend. Again, written on the eve of her death."

Restless, Margaret picked up her pencil. Not to take notes, but to draw a face. An angular face with a previously broken nose and a wide mouth.

The lawyer continued. "'To my friend Cody Ralston I leave my beloved pet, Babou. It is my dying wish that the above-mentioned Cody Ralston pose in my magazine as my first centerfold. Clothing is optional, but I believe his picture will stimulate circulation. For this service he will be paid the sum of fifty thousand dollars.'"

Margaret dropped her pencil.

Cody dropped his jaw.

"'As for my mechanic at the Main Street Garage, the chef at the diner and my cleaning lady, Rosalie, I leave one thousand dollars each, for service above and beyond the call of duty.'"

And then it was over. After most everyone else had left, Margaret stood and approached Mr. Ross.

"If I... How long do I have..." she stammered.

"Now, Margaret," he said kindly. "Don't make any hasty decisions. Come and see me anytime. We'll talk it over."

She nodded as he left the conference room, her lower lip trembling at the enormity of the choices she faced. She turned to see Cody standing at her place at the large table, looking down at her notebook with narrowed eyes.

"Uh...excuse me," she said, swooping down and snatching up the incriminating drawing. With a swift motion she wedged the notepad under her arm.

"If that was me, I'm flattered," he said sarcastically.

"It wasn't meant to be flattering," she said as the heat rushed up to color her cheeks.

"I'm flattered you cared enough to draw me," he explained with a gleam in his eye.

"What makes you think it's you?"

"The way you were staring at me." He held out his hand. "Can I have it?"

"I was not... No, absolutely not."

He raised his eyebrows, obviously surprised at being turned down. It must not happen very often. But a second later he shrugged as if he didn't care.

She picked up her briefcase and stuffed the notepad and pencil in it, then slanted a quick glance at Cody. He seemed bigger and broader today, overshadowing the whole legal office with his height, his uncombed hair and his powerful broad build. There were lines she hadn't noticed before, forking off from the corners of his eyes. Her fingers itched for her pencil to make the corrections in her sketch.

"Were you struck," he asked, "by the unusual terms of the will?"

"I shouldn't be, knowing Aunt Maud, but yes, I guess I was." She looked around at the empty office and heard the lawyer's words echo off the dark wood walls.

"What about you?" she asked. "What do you make of her offer? Had she ever mentioned posing to you before?"

They walked slowly down the stairs and out onto the street before he answered. "She asked me if I wanted to advertise. Offered me free space, not a centerfold, but I turned her down flat."

"Why?"

"It's against my principles." He put his hat on his head and added, "It's not the posing I mind, it's all those women throwing themselves at me when the magazine comes out."

Margaret squeezed her eyes shut to block the image of Cody sprawled across her aunt's magazine, wearing nothing but his hat and snug jeans. The wide shoulders, the hair on his chest, soft, yet crisp, tapering down...

She swallowed hard. "It seems to be happening anyway," she said. "All the women in town throwing themselves at you."

"*You* seem to be able to keep your distance," he noted.

"I have a lot of self-control." Or she used to. Since she'd returned to Second Chance, she couldn't seem to control her sexual fantasies—all revolving around one man, the man she almost married.

"Maybe too much," he suggested, taking the car keys out of Margaret's hand and unlocking the door of the Bronco for her.

At the touch of his hand Margaret was hit by a wave of pure, dizzy desire. She blamed it on the shock of the noonday sun after the dark cool law office, on missing breakfast, on anxiety and on her nonexistent sex life. She reached for the door handle. He beat her to it.

"So you're not going to accept the money?" she asked. "You're not going to be the first centerfold?"

"Never. I'd have fifty thousand dollars but no self-respect."

Then he put the keys in her palm and wrapped her fingers around them. His hand was large and warm and callused. She knew how it would feel if he slipped it into her lace blouse and cupped her breasts. Thank goodness he didn't know how much she yearned for his touch, *burned* for it....

"Going home?" he asked, leaning against the vehicle as she got in and closed the door.

"Of course," she answered. She was so rattled, her pulse was pounding double time and she hardly knew what she was saying.

"Because if you are, I'll come by and pick up Babou."

"Oh, oh sure. Fine. I'll give you his cage and everything.'' Relieved to be away from him if only temporarily, she headed for home as fast as she could. But it was not her home. It was her aunt's home and always would be, no matter who lived there.

Three

___

You couldn't miss Maud's house, Margaret thought. It was the only plum-colored Victorian with lavender trim set in a grove of willows on the edge of town. Cody's truck was there, but he was nowhere to be seen. Margaret walked around the house on flagstone steps, heading for the lawn that sloped down to the creek. Splashy purple tulips were clustered in raised beds, and lilac bushes lined the fence.

Every smell and sight reminded her of her flamboyant aunt. She smiled to herself as she remembered Aunt Maud's imperious voice as she stood in the middle of her garden, wearing a large hat and giving orders to her gardener.

"Perennials over here, bulbs along the borders, hanging baskets, more color!" She always knew exactly what she wanted. And now she wanted Margaret to stay in Second Chance. Why?

"So all this is yours now." Cody interrupted her thoughts. He was leaning against a white birch, watching Margaret as she approached.

She stopped, set her briefcase on the wrought-iron table under an apple tree and swallowed hard. "*Would* be mine, if I did what she said."

"Pretty stiff conditions," he agreed.

"Impossible."

"Which part?" he inquired idly while stripping a leaf from a branch of the tree.

"Every part. Running the magazine, finding a husband…" She choked back a laugh that suddenly turned into a sob. Cody's eyebrows rose, reminding her of what happened the last time she cried in front of him. She didn't want him to think she needed him. So she gripped the edge of the table and managed a quivery smile.

"So you're taking the easy way out," he said, his lip curled down at the corners.

"You think it's easy to make a living as an interior designer?" she demanded. "It's not."

"Afraid to try something new?" he asked.

She sat down with a thud in one of the wrought-iron chairs. "No, I'm not afraid to try something new. I've been trying new things ever since I left this town. Which is more than I can say for some people who are exactly the same as when I left. Same truck, same hat, same—" She stopped abruptly before she said something she'd regret. Like "same irresistible body."

"Why do you care if I go or stay?" she asked, knowing that he did care. He wanted her gone.

Cody crossed the terrace in a few large strides, yanked another chair to the table and sat across from her. "Only one reason. I… My friend needs a wife, which means we need a way to advertise for one, and *Lonesome Cowboy* is the best way to do it," he said, leaning forward to impale her with his intense blue gaze.

She edged back in her chair. "Of course it is. But you don't need me to do that. I'm sure the new owner will be happy to accommodate you. As soon as I sell the magazine, you can place your—*his* ad."

"But finding a new owner's going to take time, and frankly my friend's not as young as he used to be, and..."

"And he wants this wife to brighten his sunset years," she said caustically. "As well as pluck his chickens."

"You remembered," he said with a mocking smile.

"How could I forget?" She almost smiled back, then caught herself in time. She wouldn't give him the satisfaction. "Are you saying that you want me to stay? To sacrifice my life and my career, take up residence in a town where I no longer feel at home and run a magazine for which I have no background nor interest so your 'friend' can find a wife?"

"Not just my friend, but all the other lonely guys around here. What about your aunt? She devoted her life to helping people. Didn't any of it rub off on you?"

Margaret sat up straight and glared at him. "How dare you criticize my life and my decisions! What do you do that's so noble? Give buffalo meat to the poor and hungry?"

"At least I'm going to honor her death wish," he said.

Margaret's eyes widened. "What?"

"I've been thinking about it. Maybe I spoke too soon back there."

"You'd pose in..."

"My jeans and my hat," he said. "Not that I want to. Since I don't want a wife, it adds up to fraud, but if that's what she wanted, well, I owe her a lot. Since you've been gone, she's lent me money, given free advice..."

"She was always good at that," Margaret said, thinking of her aunt urging her to give up Cody for a career.

"What about you? Can you turn your back on your aunt's last wishes and walk out of here, after all she did for you?" He held his hand up in front of her face. "No, don't answer that. You could walk out on Mother Teresa and never look back. You've had practice. You're good at it."

She could feel the heat of anger radiate from his body. She wanted to shrink into her chair until she became invisible. But she couldn't let him affect her that way.

"Now wait a minute," she protested.

"No, *you* wait a minute. You don't have the guts to stay here for a year. You're afraid to run a magazine. Because you'll never be half the woman your aunt was, and you know it," he taunted.

"I'm not afraid to run a magazine," she countered. "I *am* afraid to lose a year out of my life. I do have a life, you know."

"Good for you. But we're talking about one year. One lousy year."

The year stretched out ahead of her like the endless highway that ran from Chicago to Second Chance, Wyoming.

"One year is long enough to lose my clients, my apartment, my...my..."

"Boyfriend?" he asked.

"No boyfriend," she admitted.

"Why not?"

She flushed as his eyes outlined the contours of her breasts under the blue suit jacket with the filmy white blouse open at the collar. She wouldn't admit she'd never met a man who measured up to him. Self-consciously she drew the lapels of the jacket together, before he could guess the effect he had on her. Before he realized her nipples were hard and peaked against her wispy lace bra.

"For someone who's cagey about what he's been doing these past six years, that's a pretty personal question," she answered.

"How have I been cagey? What do you want to know about me?"

"How come you didn't get married?"

"Ha. I tried that once. Fortunately it didn't happen."

"Fortunately?" she asked under her breath.

"Who needs to be tied down to one woman when there are so many out there? When I think of how close I came, how I almost missed out on the rich variety of experiences available to a single man around these parts..."

He propped his elbows on the table and she noticed the golden brown hairs on his arms and the way his muscles strained the cotton fabric of his shirt. She had an aching need to touch him, to slide her hands up his rock-hard chest, to feel the heat from his skin burn through his shirt to scorch her palms. Then she remembered all those other women who'd shared such a rich variety of experiences with him.

"So you've been...busy these past years," she said, a tight knot forming in her chest.

"Sure have," he said with a wicked gleam in his eye, leaving no doubt what type of experiences he was referring to. So what did she expect, that he'd stayed celibate, in honor of her memory?

She licked her lips nervously. She'd heard more than she wanted to know about his life in the past six years. Yes, she'd wondered what he'd been doing, but now she knew. She didn't want to hear any more. She didn't even want to sit across the table from him.

"Well," she said, keeping her voice steady. "If you

ever change your mind, you can always turn to *Lonesome Cowboy*."

"I'll remember that," he said.

"You're not getting any younger, you know."

"That's just what Muddy used to say."

"And your answer was...?"

"The kind of woman who'd answer an ad in *Lonesome Cowboy* is not the kind of woman I'm looking for."

"So you *were* looking."

"I was *not*," he insisted, but he grinned at her in spite of himself. The lines at the corners of his eyes crinkled and she smiled back.

For a long moment she sat opposite him under the apple blossoms with her gaze locked on his. She wished she could look away—at the tree, at the sky, or the grass. Anywhere but at this overconfident cowboy. But she couldn't.

Her smile faded as she wondered if she'd ever feel his arms around her again, ever feel his fingers sifting through her hair, or his intoxicating kisses on her lips. Not that she needed any kisses, especially the intoxicating kind. She needed to stay sober and levelheaded to make important decisions about the future of the magazine and her own future, as well.

The air grew warm, and still no one said a word. The tension built. The silence stretched like a rubber band until Cody finally spoke.

"My friend is looking," he said abruptly. "If that means anything to you. You could find him someone if you were running the magazine, couldn't you?"

"Of course." Margaret remembered her aunt's warm heart, her kindness, her devotion to her subscribers and to the whole town. How could she let them down? She stood next to the table and blinked back a tear.

Cody watched her agonize over her decision, unable to

keep from adding his two cents. "But you're not running the magazine, are you? Though it was your aunt's *dying wish*. If you leave now, without giving the magazine and Second Chance a second chance, you'll regret it," he warned. He told himself he didn't care if she stayed or went. He told himself he was being impartial. But he wasn't. He'd deny it to his dying day, but somewhere deep down inside he wanted her to give the magazine, Second Chance and *him* a second chance.

"I...I don't know what to do," she murmured.

"Forget it," he said, clenching his hands into fists. "Let the magazine fall apart. What do you care about the lonely men stuck on ranches in the middle of nowhere? Go back to Chicago. The sooner the better. That's what you want to do. My friend and all the other single guys will just have to live out their lives alone. Don't worry, you'll have your career in, what was it...interior design?" His voice was pure sarcasm.

Margaret knotted her fingers together. He made it sound so superficial, so trivial, compared to helping deserving persons find love and happiness. His face blurred before her eyes. An apple blossom wafted down and settled on her hair. There was a hush in the air while the whole world waited to hear what Margaret Kidder was going to do with her aunt's magazine and with her own life.

Cody stuffed his hands in his back pockets and stared at Margaret. She was so damned beautiful, so totally out of place here in her tailored suit. Despite the apple blossom in her hair, she'd turned strictly big-city with her briefcase and high heels. Why on earth should he ever urge her to stay when she'd just leave at the last minute like she did before?

For Jake, he told himself. For Jake's sake. Without Margaret the magazine would fold. She was kidding herself if she thought she could sell the magazine. Who would move to Second Chance to run a lonely hearts magazine? Nobody. It had to be someone who knew the area, who knew the people and the life-style. It had to be Margaret. Without Margaret there was no *Lonesome Cowboy* and without *Lonesome Cowboy* there was no wife for Jake.

Margaret took a step forward, waiting for him to say something. She was so close, he saw temptation in her eyes. Temptation to go, or temptation to stay, or temptation to fly into his arms?

What would happen if he kissed her? Just one kiss before she left for good. She might not mind. But he might not be able to stop. Might lose control. And Cody Ralston was always in control. Ever since that day he stood on Main Street in the rain, watching her bus disappear down the highway, he'd never let go of his emotions.

He could hear Aunt Maud's voice now. *Cody,* she'd say, *keep your hands off Margaret. Yes, I want her to run the magazine. And I want you for my first centerfold. But these are strictly business decisions. Don't think I'm trying to throw you together. Margaret doesn't belong here anymore. She needs a penthouse apartment, not an isolated ranch house in the middle of nowhere. Yes, she needs a husband and you need a wife, but that doesn't mean...*

He cut off the voice in his head by reaching for the apple blossom in her hair. If he got rid of that flower he could certainly get rid of Margaret. Get her out of his mind and out of his dreams. Yes, okay, he'd dreamed about her. But not since last night. All it meant was that he'd been too long without a woman.

He watched while she drew a shaky breath and closed her eyes. As if she thought he was going to kiss her. Which he was not. Her lips were full and desirable. He knew what she'd taste like. Sunshine and roses. He knew

what she'd feel like in his arms. Like she belonged there.
But he couldn't, he shouldn't and he *wouldn't*.

"If you do decide to stay," he said brusquely, "I'll tell
you who my friend is. I don't think he'll mind."

Her eyes flew open and she teetered backward in her
Italian leather shoes. "Really?" she asked, biting back her
disappointment. Nothing had happened. No kiss. Nothing.

"I think you'll remember him."

"I'm sure I will," she said politely. "Why don't you
bring him into the office?" she suggested. "Oh, I forgot,
he's shy."

"Yes, he is. But there's gotta be a way. You free on
Sunday?"

"Probably not," she said, brushing a speck of dust off
her skirt. "What for?"

"A barbecue. *To celebrate my birthday.* At the ranch.
I'll pick you up at noon."

"I'll drive myself."

He pointed his finger at her, coming close to touching
her left breast just over her heart. "Be there," he instructed. Then he ambled off around the house without
another word, and Margaret exhaled a giant sigh of relief.

She pressed her hand over her heart and stood staring
into space, listening to the sound of his truck cough and
sputter. She didn't realize she was holding her breath until
the engine caught and raced, and finally accelerated down
the long driveway. Thank heavens he was gone. It took
her about fifteen minutes before she realized he'd forgotten Babou. She hoped he wouldn't come back for him.
She'd rather cope with a dangerous animal than a smart-
aleck cowboy any day.

Sunday was a hazy spring day, the early-morning sunshine already hinting of warm summer days to come.
Cody gulped bitter coffee and watched, from the kitchen

window, as the men set up the barbecue stands, wishing he'd never allowed the crew to give him a birthday party, especially at his house, especially today.

He wasn't in the mood for a party. He wasn't in the mood to celebrate the end of his thirty-first year of life and with it the realization that his big gamble on buffalo might not pay off. And if it didn't, everyone in town would say, "I told you so." To top it off, the girl who'd dumped him six years ago had come back as a woman. A mature, sexy, desirable woman, come back to remind him of what he'd missed.

And today he could look forward to entertaining said woman along with the whole community, who would joke and speculate about his prospects even as they wolfed down his charbroiled buffalo steaks. What had compelled him to invite *her?* Then he remembered: Jake.

And where was Jake? He dumped the remains of his coffee into the sink and went out to the bunkhouse, where he found his foreman doubled up on his bed with a mound of blankets on top of him despite the rising thermometer.

"Good God, what's wrong with you?" Cody asked, staring wide-eyed at his friend.

"Don't know. Got the shakes and the chills," he said, his teeth chattering wildly.

"What can I get you?" Cody asked, his forehead wrinkled in concern. "Coffee, tea...what?"

Jake shook his head. "Can't eat. Sorry about your birthday."

"Forget my birthday. We gotta get you well. I'm calling Doc Weston."

"Dusty already did. He'll take a look when he comes out to the party."

"*He's* coming to the party, too?" Did they leave anyone out?

Instead of answering, Jake moaned and covered his

head with his pillow. Cody stared at Jake for a long helpless moment, then he slammed his hand against his forehead. "Be back later," he said over his shoulder as he
ran back to the house, snatched the receiver off the
kitchen wall and punched in Maud's home number. Her
phone rang and rang and finally her voice told him she
was temporarily away from home and would he please
leave a message.

Cody froze at the sound of Maud's voice. It made a
chill go up his spine, thinking of her speaking to him from
beyond. Then he dialed the office of *Lonesome Cowboy*
and got a similar message. What was wrong with her niece
that she couldn't replace those recorded messages? And
where was Margaret? Gone back to Chicago hopefully.
But just in case, he sent her an urgent telepathic message.
*Don't come, don't come, don't come. The man is sick,
sick, sick.*

She didn't receive the messages. Or if she did, she came
anyway. He saw her out of the corner of his eye from
where he was tending bar at the edge of the corral. He
thought about crossing the patio and greeting her, intro-
ducing her around. But this was Margaret, accustomed to
gallery openings, cocktail parties and the like. She didn't
need him. For anything.

Still, he couldn't keep his eyes off her as he continued
to mix drinks and some other guy, some neighbor, took
the opportunity to greet her and make sure she got a buffalo steak.

He saw her eyes scan the crowd, as if she was looking
for his friend, then she looked across the ragged lawn and
her eyes met his. His mouth went dry as a cottonwood
tree as he wondered if she remembered the last time she'd
been there. The night before the wedding. The night the

earth shook and nothing was ever the same again. The night they made love.

When he finally made his way over to her, he found her seated smack-dab in the middle of a bench pulled up to a picnic table lined on both sides by hungry males all wolfing down his barbecued meat. When Jack Harkins got up to refill his plate with potato salad and baked beans, Cody wedged himself into his place on the picnic bench.

"Nice you could come," he remarked as casually as he could, considering his thigh was pressed against hers, causing an erratic increase in his heart rate. She turned her face in his direction and he drew in a deep breath. Dear heaven, she was so lovely, even with the smear of barbecue sauce on the corner of her mouth. If he leaned forward just an inch or so...

"Where *is* he?" she asked in a low tone while the rowdy conversation continued around them.

"That's right, don't waste time on pleasantries. Get to the point," he said. "I don't think you've wished me a happy birthday yet."

"Happy Birthday," she said. "I left your present in the car."

"Why, is it personal?"

"Not the way you mean it."

"Something I've always wanted?"

"Something you asked me for, but I didn't give it to you."

"Then it couldn't be..."

"No, it couldn't."

She was so close, her elusive scent wrapped around him and threatened to hold him prisoner. "Good God, Margaret, stop it. Give it to me or stop talking about it."

"Let's talk about your friend."

Cody took a deep breath. "He's sick."

She nodded, her lips pursed together. "I'm not surprised. What does he have, some rare wasting disease that he needs a wife to take care of him?"

"He's got the flu," Cody said under his breath.

"Is it a secret?" Margaret asked.

"I told you he doesn't want anyone to know."

"I know what you told me. But the story keeps changing."

"It does not change," he muttered. "But I may have left out a few details. One…"

"Since he's not here, couldn't we do this in my office?" she asked.

"*'My office,'*" he quoted. "Does that mean you're staying?"

"I guess I'm staying…if you're posing."

He grinned at her. "You wouldn't want to miss that, would you?"

Margaret flushed the color of the sauce she'd dribbled on her chin. "I just meant that if you're going to honor her death wish, then I feel obliged to do the same. But there's more."

"I thought so," he said.

"The idea of selling the magazine was like selling a member of the family. For as long as I can remember there was Aunt Maud and me and the magazine. Considering how little there is left of our family, I just couldn't do it. Honestly, I don't know how I…" Yes, she didn't know *how* she…and *why* she ever considered it. But now that she'd made her decision, it seemed obvious it was the right thing to do. Did it have anything to do with the fact that she wasn't the roaring success as an interior designer she thought she'd be? Or did it have something to do with Cody? That was another matter. One she'd think about later. Much later. When he wasn't around to distract her with his sexy banter and his dazzling blue eyes.

He took his index finger and wiped her lower lip so that she never finished her sentence. "My friend will be grateful to you. Because he knows as well as I know that without you the magazine would go under. And he'd never find Miss Right. There isn't anyone on this earth who could run it as well as you.''

''You think so?'' she asked, soaking up his rare kind words like a sponge.

''I know so. Hey, why don't we go see how he's doing, maybe take him a piece of cake?'' he asked. Finally she'd get to meet Jake. And see how deserving he was. And realize how important it was that she stay.

She shrugged as if it didn't matter one way or the other, but it mattered to him. Just in case there was a lingering doubt in her mind. The sight of Jake doubled up on his bunk, with a raging fever, would erase that doubt forever. And he didn't want anyone, especially Margaret, to question his veracity.

Forgetting all about the cake, he led the way past the fiddlers just tuning up, through the smoke from the barbecue and around the back of the barn to the bunkhouse. Cody opened the door and peered into the dim interior. Jake's bed was empty. Margaret was behind him, so close, she almost stepped on his heels. He turned and she ran into him as the door slammed behind her.

They stood there, with his hands braced on her shoulders for a long moment. He hadn't planned on kissing her when he'd invited her. But the memory of her mouth, her sweet hot kisses tormented him. And now they were alone, and she was so close, he could see the flecks of green in her eyes, feel the heat from her body right through her shirt. He had to do it. His mouth closed over hers.

He wasn't going to punish her. He was going to seduce her. Make her want him the way he wanted her. With heated kisses and whispered urgings he turned up the heat.

She felt it. With a deep sigh, and a sensual moan from

the back of her throat, she invited him in. To taste, to give, to take.

He groaned with pleasure when she opened to him. And drank her in as if he'd been lost in the desert for days. With his hands on her hips he molded her to his body, so close they felt like one. So close, his arousal made it clear what he wanted. Wanted her body pressed against his— ready, willing and so turned on, she'd be unable to stop herself or him.

But she was able to stop. With a jagged sigh she broke away and looked over his shoulder. "Where is he?" she asked, the catch in her voice the only indication she was anywhere near as aroused as he was.

So she wanted to play it cool? Well, he could be as cool as anyone, provided no one noticed the increase in his heartbeat.

"Gone," he said, dropping his arms to his sides.

"I guess he wasn't as sick as you thought he was," she said.

He glared at her. "He must be in the house."

She turned and opened the door. He strode ahead of her toward the back of his house and flung the door open. Margaret followed him into the kitchen and looked around, studying the faded curtains and the worn lino-leum.

"Ever think of redecorating this place?" she asked.

"No." Where was Jake?

"I always thought this room had possibilities," she said looking at the open shelves crammed with chipped cups and jelly glasses.

"Yeah. Uh-huh."

Her eyes lit up at the sight of his grandmother's dish cabinet. "I'd like to get my hands on an old hutch like that," she said.

"I'd like to get my hands on that guy," he muttered.

"Have you thought about an island unit?" she inquired.

"I'm too busy thinking about something else."

"Interior design doesn't have to be expensive. It's basically just manipulating space."

He leaned against the scarred pinewood counter and observed her with narrowed eyes. "I'll bet you're good at that."

"Actually, I don't usually do kitchens."

"What do you do? Studios, game rooms, foyers?" he asked, still aching with unfulfilled lust.

"Bedrooms are my specialty," she confessed. Then boldly her gaze met his. "Could we look at yours?"

"I hope you know what you're doing," he warned.

She smiled a sweet seductive smile. Standing there in his kitchen with the sun picking up amber glints in her rich chestnut hair, she was all round-eyed innocence. *Sure she was.*

She was mad, crazy, out of her mind if she thought he'd take her into his bedroom. As if he hadn't been punished enough. The memory of making love to her there had tormented him for weeks, months, years. He remembered too well how it felt to bury himself inside her welcoming heat. To hear her cry out. To lie together as their passion cooled only to heat up again and again.

Obviously he was a glutton for punishment. Because before he could think, he heard himself say, "Right this way."

Four

His bedroom was paneled in dark wood. The sliding door to the double closet stood open and a pile of unfolded, unironed clean clothes threatened to tumble out into the room. The wastebasket overflowed. Margaret inhaled deeply. The smell was leather and tobacco and pure Cody. She tried to avoid looking at the bed, but there it was, huge and unmade, rumpled striped sheets and pillows tossed every which way. What had possessed her to come into this room? She wrapped her arms around her waist, fighting the onslaught of memories. She reminded herself she was there as a decorator, not a lover. *Former* lover.

But she couldn't help remembering how sweet his kisses were, how tender his touch, how loving the words he whispered in her ear. All that from this hardened, rough-edged cowboy who stood across the room looking at her as if she were an alien life form come to invade his universe, instead of a decorator come to redo his bedroom.

"Yes," she said, keeping her voice brisk and professional while her heart beat in time to a frantic rhythm. "It needs work."

Cody rested his hands on his hips and regarded her through narrowed eyes. "What did you have in mind?"

In mind? She had in mind what happened in that bed next to the window. The bed she couldn't keep her eyes off. It lured her, beckoned to her, to give it—and him—another try, just for old times' sake.

She couldn't look at Cody without thinking about that tumultuous night six years ago, and she couldn't look at his bed. But she was quickly running out of places to look. "You need more light," she said, glancing in desperation at the ceiling. "A skylight would be perfect in here."

"Where?"

"Over the bed."

"No way. What if it leaks? Right in the middle of…"

"It won't."

"If it does, will you replace the…"

"The sheets? Of course."

"That's not what I was going to say," he said, leaning against the bedpost with a gleam in his eye. "If a woman got rained on, it might dampen her…enthusiasm. So I'd need a replacement. Can I count on you?"

"You can count on me for my professional services," she said stiffly.

"That's all?" He shook his head. "I should have known. Nothing's changed."

"Everything's changed and you know it," Margaret said, raising her chin. "I left here a naive and innocent girl…."

"Innocent? You call yourself innocent after what happened in this room? Or have you forgotten?" he demanded, his eyes dark and dangerous.

"I haven't forgotten how nice you were to me then,

how considerate, how generous, how, how…'' She trailed
off and bit her lip. She wouldn't cry. She *would not.*
''Don't say you haven't changed,'' she said walking
across the varnished oak floor until they were face-to-face,
eyeball-to-eyeball. ''You haven't said a civil word to me
since I got here. You've done nothing but criticize my
career choice, told me no one in town cares about me,
implied that I left because I was afraid of hard work and
made it clear you despise me.''

The taut lines around his mouth softened almost imperceptibly. ''I don't despise you,'' he said gruffly.

''No? Well I'd hate to see how you treat someone you
do despise. You'd probably put them through your shred-
der and use them for mulch.''

A glimmer of warmth shone in the depths of his eyes.
He traced a line around the curve of her cheek with one
finger. ''I'd never do that to you, Margaret,'' he said
softly.

She drew a shaky breath, wishing she'd never mentioned how he'd changed. If he started being kind and
sweet again, she'd have no defense against him. She'd be
putty in his hands. He'd try to talk her into staying in
Second Chance forever, just like the last time she was in
this room.

She took a deep breath, determined to keep the conversation light. ''Well, that's a relief. But would you feed
me into the hay baler and leave me in the fields till fall?''
she asked.

He tilted her chin with his thumb and studied her face
as if he'd never seen it before. ''Uh-huh,'' he said absently. ''Not a bad idea.''

''Which one?'' she asked, her voice catching as his
callused thumb stroked a trail along the neckline of her
shirt and paused at the valley between her breasts. Tiny

goose bumps rose on her skin and her knees shook. It was her fault. She should never have come into this room.

"About the skylight."

"Really? You mean it? You know it would really lighten up the room," she said, taking a step backward and looking at the ceiling again.

"Tell me again where it would go," he said.

Impatiently she grabbed his arm and dragged him across the room to the side of the bed. She pointed to an area directly above his pillows. "There."

He frowned. "I don't know. I can't picture it."

"Oh, for heaven's sake. Lie down and look up."

"By myself?"

She looked at him for a long moment. Did he think, for one moment, that she was going to lie next to him in *that* bed? Yes, he did. It was there in his insolent gaze, that cocky, damn-I'm-good attitude that characterized the new Cody Ralston. She remembered only too clearly the series of women who'd thrown themselves at him at the saloon that day. And had most certainly been throwing themselves at him for the past six years. No wonder he was so...self-assured.

Margaret exhaled loudly. "I realize a man like you is seldom in bed by himself, but maybe just this once, in the interest of interior design, you wouldn't mind...."

"I *would* mind. I can't lie there by myself and imagine a skylight over my head. If you're any kind of decorator, you'll help me visualize it. Unless you feel your emotions will get in the way. That's it, isn't it? You don't trust yourself in bed with me." He gave her a knowing smile that made her blood boil.

"You really think you're some hotshot cowboy, don't you? But you're not as irresistible as you think."

"I'm not?" he asked. "Prove it." He jumped onto the bed, lay on his back and crossed his arms under his head.

Then he waited with a wolfish grin on his face she would have been crazy to ignore. On the other hand, she *was* a professional. And if the client wanted her to explain the advantages of a skylight from the vantage point of beneath the skylight…

She rubbed her damp palms against her khaki slacks, took a deep breath and very gingerly slid onto the bed and lay as close to the edge as she could without falling off. But even then he was too close. She knew he was looking at her; she felt the heat from his gaze, felt the challenge to show him she was immune to his charms, while all the time her treacherous body wanted him next to her, on top of her, inside of her, until there was no distance between them at all and they were one. Two halves of a whole. Together again.

He attracted her as he always had. In the most primitive way. A way she couldn't ignore. Despite his insults, she wanted to straddle his body, unbutton his shirt and let her hair cascade over his shoulders. Let her hands skim over his bare chest, showing him she remembered what he liked. Make him groan with pleasure and plead for mercy. She wanted to unbutton his snug, well-worn jeans and stroke and tantalize his masculinity until he was at the brink of ecstasy. And then…and then…

She gripped handfuls of striped sheet to stop the insistent flow of desire that raced through her veins. She stared at the white plaster ceiling as if it was the most fascinating ceiling she'd ever seen. He was right. Her emotions were getting in the way. Along with her memories. Bittersweet memories of their last night together, the rain on the roof, her breasts pressed against his hard chest, his hands lifting her into the cradle of his thighs.

She remembered the things he said in the heat of passion. The things he didn't say. The things they did. The things they didn't do—things they were saving for their wedding night. The night that never came. So much was left unsaid. So much was left undone. Warm, confused, aching feelings washed over her, and hot tears threatened to spill out onto the sheets.

"See," he said, startling her out of her reverie, "how irresistible I am?"

She nodded without turning her head and swallowed her tears. It was time to face the fact that her memories were all she had and all she ever would have. Cody was a different person from the man she once knew and she was different, too. It was too late for them. It had been too late from the minute she'd turned and run out of the church.

The three feet that separated them on that bed were a symbol of the distance that separated their lives. It was time to pull herself together and show him how professional she could be. To show him she hadn't been wasting her time these past six years. She cleared her throat. "I'm wondering if six by eight would be too big," she said. "They come in different sizes."

"What does?" he asked.

"Skylights. Isn't that what this is about?"

She suddenly realized that while she was looking at the ceiling, he'd closed the gap between them and had propped his head in his hand to look down at her. "Is it?" he asked, his face so close, she could see pinpoints of light in the depths of his eyes. She felt desire rise once again, somewhere deep within her, and threaten to overwhelm her. But was it anger or passion that smoldered in his gaze? She couldn't tell. "Or is it about you and me?" he demanded.

With an effort, she raised her head and leveled a cool gaze at him. "There is no you and me."

"No?" It was the kind of challenge Cody never could resist. He'd seen reluctant desire in Margaret's eyes. He'd heard it in her voice. The only way to convince her there *was* a "you and me," was to *show* her. He lowered his mouth until it was just a whisper away from hers. He gave her a millisecond to turn her head or push him away. She didn't.

What else could he do? He claimed her with a kiss, a fierce, ferocious kiss that burned its way clear to the heels of his boots. Hotter than any kiss in his past, hotter than the spicy barbecue sauce that lingered on her lips. He hoped it showed her something, because it sure as hell showed him there was still something between them. Especially when she rolled over on top of him and pressed scorching eager kisses over his face. He opened his mouth and welcomed her tongue to dance and tangle with his. His breath was as rapid and ragged as hers.

Her silky hair spilled over onto his shoulders, and the scent of hothouse roses mingled with the smell of fresh hay that wafted in from the open window. He yanked his shirt out of his jeans, wanting to get rid of everything between them, every scrap of fabric, and mold her to him, shoulder to thigh, to feel her warm soft skin against his, her rich full curves filling every hollow of his body.

He reached under her soft knit shirt and cupped her breasts in his broad palms. Marveling at how well she fit. As if he'd forgotten.

He heard her shocked gasp of pleasure as he stroked her nipples with his thumbs. She gripped his arms and a flood of memories came pounding back. No matter how else she'd changed, she was still so incredibly responsive. "It's been so long," he muttered, his lips pressed against her cheek.

"Too long," she murmured, struggling to unbutton his shirt. Then she caught herself. She lifted her chin and looked at him. He saw both passion and denial simmering in the depths of her eyes. "Cody, we can't do this," she breathed.

"We *are* doing it," he said, rolling to one side and taking her with him.

Raucous voices came from far in the distance. Music wafted through the warm spring air.

"There's a party going on out there," she said breathlessly, her heart beating in time to his.

"I like the one in here better," he said.

Her lips curved just slightly and he realized how much he'd missed her smile. How much he wanted to make her smile again, and laugh again and love again. But that was not going to happen. The only thing that was going to happen was he was going to take advantage of the moment. This moment when he had Margaret to himself, in his bed. He was going to take advantage of her as she'd taken advantage of him. And then he was going to leave her as she'd left him. Finally she'd feel what he felt. Alone.

He braced her head with his hand and laced his fingers through her hair. He meant to bruise her with more fierce kisses, but when his lips met hers they turned tender instead. What was wrong with him? It was her. It was her cloud of dark hair, her warm, caramel-colored eyes, and her body pressed against his. He couldn't stay far enough away from her and he couldn't get close enough, either. He hated to admit it, but he wanted her now more than he'd ever wanted her before. He groaned with frustration and need and pulled her shirt off over her head. In a flash he unsnapped her bra and tossed it over the side of the bed.

Margaret fought to catch her breath. His tongue was hot and wet as it teased and stroked the nubs of her nipples, first one, then the other. She felt her breasts swell to fit the contours of his hands. She was so exquisitely sensitive to his touch. Too much was happening too fast. And yet it wasn't enough. Or fast enough. Her whole body throbbed with desire. She wanted him. All of him. It was the reason she'd come to his bedroom. Not to see his bedroom, but to see him, to touch him, to love him.

She fumbled for the buttons on his shirt again, ripping the last two in her rush to lay her hands against the flat planes of his chest, revel in dark hair there.

He returned the favor by unzipping her slacks with one hand and throwing them over the side of the bed to join her bra in a heap on the floor. She rolled onto her back and he braced his hands against hers, pinning her against the firm mattress. His heated gaze questioned her, gave her one last chance to say no before it was too late.

But it was too late minutes ago, hours ago, years ago. She was destined to make love with Cody one more time. She knew it and he knew it. Satisfied with the answer in her eyes, he released her hands and bent over to trail hot kisses along the border of her silk bikinis. Molten lava, hot and thick, pooled in the very core of her being. Then he removed the scrap of beige silk panties, too, tossed aside with everything else. She fought off a flush of embarrassment as she lay naked to his fevered gaze. Everything was gone but his jeans. And she noticed them growing tighter by the minute.

He ignored his own discomfort to dip his mouth lower, past the silky curls, tantalizing and teasing her. The painful pleasure built until she was on the brink of madness. It had been so long, too long. When she thought she would surely die of this exquisite torture, his tongue found the nub of her desire, the center of her being. The world spun around and she called his name, pleading, demanding release. With one last stroke of his tongue she gave up everything to him.

In return, an earth-shaking explosion streaked through

her, shattering her into a million pieces. Leaving her shaken, defenseless and wanting more. More than physical release. She wanted love, but she'd never admit it. Cody stared down at her, a certain triumph in his eyes. He looked strangely satisfied, but he couldn't be, not until...

"My turn," she whispered huskily and put her hands on his hips to peel his jeans off. It was way past time those jeans came off. With shaking fingers she worked at the rivets, feeling the strength and size of his arousal through the denim.

And then it happened. The voices at the door, the relentless pounding.

"Come on out, Cody. We know you're in there. It's time to blow out the candles. And make a wish."

"Go away. That's my wish," Cody muttered, jumping out of bed and stuffing his arms into the sleeves of his shirt.

"Hiding out in your room won't solve anything," a man's voice said. "You'll still be thirty-two when you come out."

"Not if I stay all year. I'll be thirty-three," he yelled.

Chills racing up and down her spine, Margaret grabbed her clothes, ran to the adjoining bathroom and closed the door behind her. A second later, she opened it and stuck her head out. "We should never have come in here," she whispered.

"Where should we have gone, to a haystack in the barn?" Cody demanded under his breath. "It was your idea, remember? 'Bedrooms are my specialty,'" he mimicked.

Her face flushed to the roots of her tousled hair. This time she shot him a venomous look before she slammed the bathroom door.

Cody stood in the middle of the room, his shirt hanging

out over his jeans, staring at the bedroom door. When he finally opened it, his shirt was tucked in, his hair was combed and he'd achieved a certain degree of acceptance. He accepted the fact that he was thirty-two. He accepted the fact that Margaret was as sexy, as responsive and as maddening as ever. And he accepted the fact that he was as frustrated, unfulfilled and disturbed as ever. And was likely to remain so.

Unless he really did order the skylight. And she had to supervise the installation. And test it in a rainstorm. It was worth it if it got her out from under his skin. He knew now the only way to do that was to make love to her. Just once would do it. Then he could turn his back on her. Even if she was in town for a year, running the magazine. She could stay for years for all he cared, growing old and withered, her hair turning gray.

Yes, that would be something to see, he thought. Margaret old and wrinkled. The thought brought a smile to his lips and a pang of longing to his heart. He shrugged off the sudden emotion, but he couldn't help wondering why the thought of growing old with Margaret held so much appeal.

Later, as he said goodbye to his guests, he watched her walk to her car without even acknowledging him. It was the first time he'd seen her since she disappeared into the bathroom.

"Hey wait a minute," he shouted, crossing the driveway. He stuck his head into the driver's side window of her car. "About the skylight."

"Yes?"

"I want to go ahead with it."

"Are you sure?"

"Unless you're not up to the challenge. Unless you want to back out. It wouldn't surprise me."

She bit her lip and turned the key in the ignition. "I'll

make some drawings and get back to you," she said. "And whenever your friend gets well, if you really have a friend, I'll try to get him in the May issue."

"Yes, I have a friend. Ask anybody. By the way, where's my present?"

She thrust a flat envelope tied with a red ribbon into his hands. Without hesitating, she put the vehicle in gear and drove off, leaving him staring after her. He'd never understand her. Not if *he* turned old and gray and lived to be one hundred.

When Margaret got back to her aunt's house, she changed into a sweatshirt, baggy sweats and threw her slacks, shirt, bikinis and bra into the clothes hamper as if they'd been contaminated with industrial waste. Every time she thought about her having said, "Bedrooms are my specialty," she felt like curling up and dying of shame. To say nothing of her disgraceful behavior that followed. And she *still* didn't know if he was wearing boxers or nothing at all. As if she cared.

Next time she would not take off her clothes until he did, she would not give up control until *he* did.... *Next time?* Was she crazy? There would be no next time. As for the skylight, she would order the materials, hire the carpenters and supervise that project from afar. Very, very far. From the office of *Lonesome Cowboy,* five miles away.

No wonder Cody had no respect for her. Every time he taunted, tempted or nagged her to do something, she did it. Beginning with promising to run the magazine to ending up in his bed today. Now she was going to remodel his bedroom. The man had her wrapped around his little finger. If she was going to spend the next year in Second Chance, she'd better unwrap herself. From now on, all their meetings would take place on neutral ground. The office, for example.

Then she thought about their meeting in the office—how he'd caused her blood pressure to go up just by glancing at her neckline, tying her sweater around her waist, brushing her cheek with the back of his hand. Her pulse raced as she remembered how he removed his hat from her head. Threaded his fingers through her hair. The clean masculine smell of his shirt, his hair and his skin had filled the office and lingered long after he left.

No, the office wouldn't do for a meeting place. It was too small, too intimate.

The saloon, then. The saloon where he'd made it clear he was the town stud who'd lost no time pining for her. Yes, the saloon, on Ladies' Night. She'd be in no danger of falling under his spell with so many other women to distract him. He'd have no time to challenge her, taunt her or insult her. Let him insult the rest of the female population of Second Chance for a change. While she signed up customers for the magazine.

That's my girl, said the ghostly voice of her aunt, reverberating softly off the high ceiling of the Victorian parlor. *Now you're getting the idea. And don't forget about Babou.*

Margaret winced. She *had* forgotten about Babou. She'd forgotten to give him to Cody. Margaret jumped up off the chintz-covered sofa and walked quickly to the back of the house to the solarium that overlooked the garden and the brook. In the corner of the room, in the specially built terrarium with a huge gnarled tree trunk, crushed bark and a saucer of water, was Babou, Aunt Maud's six-foot-long boa constrictor.

Margaret switched on the light over the terrarium and froze. The enclosure was empty. The screen that formed the lid was gnawed away at one corner and Babou was gone. Panic rose in her throat. She fought off the urge to jump up on a wicker table and scream. No one would hear her except Babou, and it might frighten him into coming out and biting her.

She drew a ragged breath. A huge, dangerous snake was loose in the house. Her gaze swept the room. Nothing was out of place. Every flowered cushion on every wicker chair, every book in the rattan bookcase, was in order. Just as her aunt had left it. Feeling foolish, she called his name. "Babou, come back here this minute, do you hear?"

Maybe he heard. Maybe he didn't. Maybe he was hiding. Maybe he was looking for something to eat. She hadn't fed him since she'd arrived. But Aunt Maud had told her she only fed him once a month, and then she gave him a live rodent. Margaret shuddered at the thought. Why hadn't she given him to Cody the day he came to get him? Why did she let Cody distract her? Why didn't she call him right now to help her find him? After all, Babou belonged to him.

She took the receiver from the old-fashioned wall phone and dialed Cody's number. After all these years, it came back to her as if it was her own. When he answered, she blurted the news.

"Have you looked everywhere?" he asked.

"I haven't looked anywhere. I'm afraid I'll find him. Boa constrictors can swallow horses and cattle whole, you know."

"That's a rumor. Besides, you don't look anything like a horse or a cow," he assured her.

"That's the nicest thing you've said to me since I came back. How do you know anyway? Are you a snake? Besides, I'm more worried about being squeezed to death or bitten. Have you ever seen their teeth? They're pointed inward." She shivered inside her sweatshirt. "And I don't care what you say, they *can* eat animals bigger than they are, because the bones of their jaws can be stretched. I read that somewhere. Their whole bodies can be stretched to accommodate their victim. And when they're finished there's nothing left but feathers and hair." The breeze ruffled the curtain at the window and Margaret screamed.

"What is it? Did you find him?" Cody said, alarmed.

"No, no. It was…something else," she said, balling her hands into fists.

"Get hold of yourself, Margaret. When he gets hungry he'll come back."

"He'll come back and get me. He hates me. I know he does."

Cody exhaled loudly and impatiently. "What do you want me to do?"

"Come over here and help me find him. He's yours, you know."

"All right," he said, and hung up.

He didn't want to see Margaret again today. He'd had as much of her tempting presence as he could take for one day. The vision of her sprawled on his bed with her head on his pillow was going to haunt him for days. While she'd probably already forgotten what happened.

If she'd called because she wanted to see him, because she wanted to finish what they'd started, he'd be there like a shot. He sighed. She only wanted him to find the snake. And for some reason, he couldn't say no.

When he arrived, she was pacing back and forth in front of the house in the twilight. She rushed to his truck and threw her arms around him when he got out. He held his arms stiffly at his side, remembering how she'd made him suffer. Keeping his body rigid, he said dryly, "Now I know how it feels to be crushed by a boa constrictor."

Her face fell, she dropped her arms and took a step backward. "I'm sorry, but I'm scared. I can't help it."

"Okay, let's get this over with," he said as he brushed past her and headed for the front door.

She followed him into the living room, sticking as close as a shadow. They opened every closet door, explored every room, every cupboard, every shelf, every drawer, Margaret stood carefully behind Cody in case the reptile leapt out with his teeth bared. Then they went upstairs and looked into Margaret's bedroom.

With a shock of recognition, he realized it was exactly the same as it had been six years ago—girlish ruffled curtains at the window and a canopy over the bed. Her stuffed animals on a shelf on the wall. Paintings and faded sketches on the wall with her distinctive *MEK* in each corner. Pictures of him on a bulletin board. Pictures of them. Why didn't she take them down? He didn't want to see them. He kneeled on the floor to look under the bed.

"I know what you're going to say," she said. "The room needs work."

"I was going to say there's no snake under the bed."

"What about the closet?"

He crawled out from under the bed, stood and walked to the closet. There was no snake there, either.

They went from room to room, and when they'd been everywhere else they propped a ladder under the trapdoor and climbed up into the musty, dusty attic.

By the light from the one bare bulb, Cody could see the snake wasn't there. Unless he was hiding in the old steamer trunk in the corner. The rusty hinges squeaked as he lifted the lid and peered inside.

Margaret laughed nervously. "You don't really think a snake could open a trunk, do you?"

Cody turned abruptly to glare at her. "I don't know what they can do. I'm just trying to put your mind at ease.

We've looked everywhere else. I can't stay here all night. I've got...things to do.''

"I'm sorry. If you'd taken him the other day..." she said.

"If you'd brought him with you to the party..." he countered.

Her gaze toured the sloped ceiling and lingered on the cobwebs in the corners. "Oh, yes, the party."

"Having second thoughts about what happened?" he asked. He knew the answer to that one. He just wanted to see what she'd say.

"Should I?"

He shrugged. "That's up to you."

"I should have known you wouldn't let me forget it," she said, her hands on her hips, her chin set at a defiant angle.

The memory of her riding the wave of passion there on his bed set his blood pumping double time through his whole body.

Their eyes met, and their thoughts tangled. The tension rose and filled the air as they both got caught up in memories, scenes, feelings. With their gazes locked, they played chicken until she gave in, tore her eyes away and then drew a deep breath. "I love old attics, don't you?" she asked.

Instead of answering, he pulled a sheet off of an easel that held a pile of canvases. "What's this?"

She grabbed the sheet out of his hands. "Just some old pictures. Aunt Maud thought if she saved my paintings they'd be worth a fortune someday."

"Do you still paint?"

She shook her head. "I'm not any good. I found that out the minute I got to Chicago. Do you know how many artists—talented artists—there are in this world who are washing dishes for a living?"

"But you used to love it. You had your easel set up in the sun room."

"I was too dumb to know I didn't have any talent."

"None? I don't believe that. You drew that picture of me."

"All right, so I have some talent. For caricatures maybe. But when I went into interior design, I gave away my paints. I grew up and got serious."

"What do you do for fun?"

She didn't have an answer for that one. Maybe she hadn't been having much fun.

Instead of answering, she reached into the trunk, pulled out an old photo album and leafed through it as if he wasn't there. It was clear he'd asked too many uncomfortable questions. In the dim light he studied her face, the delicate curve of her cheekbone, the fine line of her eyebrows. Even looking at her in her shapeless sweatshirt and pants made him ache with an old longing. He saw her lower lip tremble as she looked at the pictures. He didn't want to know why. He wanted to find the snake and go home.

Instead, he moved behind her to look over her shoulder. "What is it?" he asked.

"My parents," she said. "And me."

In the faded photograph, a young woman in bell-bottom pants held a little girl in her arms while a tall young man smiled proudly at them. A big Wyoming sky formed the backdrop and the date was written below in Maud's flowery handwriting.

"You were a beautiful baby," Cody blurted. So beautiful, he had to close his eyes for a minute. A brief vision of how a child of theirs might look intruded on his consciousness and threatened to destroy his hard-won peace of mind.

She turned her head toward him so her face was just a

breath away. Her eyes glistened. "I was two years old here. The year they died. Do you know, I don't remember them. And that makes me sad."

Instinctively Cody put his hand on her shoulder and massaged gently, forgetting he'd vowed never to touch her again. "Look how happy they are. They wouldn't want you to be sad."

"I know. I know. They were so much in love. You can tell, can't you?"

"They had it all," Cody agreed. "Each other and you, too."

Margaret pressed her lips together and nodded, but a tear trickled down her cheek.

Without thinking, Cody brushed it away with the pad of his thumb. He watched her swallow hard, and something stirred inside him—some buried emotion he did not want to deal with. He did not want to rub his thumb over the taut tendons of her neck, easing her sorrow. He didn't want to feel the pulse that pounded in the hollow of her throat, because it would be the end of him.

He dropped his arms to his sides, took a step backward and looked her over. Her gray sweat suit hung shapelessly from her shoulders and the sweatpants bagged and bunched at the ankles. Her hair was a tangle of snarls and there was a smudge of dirt on her forehead. She looked like a refugee from a war zone, and it suddenly occurred to him for the first time that he might never get over her in this lifetime. And that scared the living hell out of him.

Margaret's tearful gaze met his just for a second; then she closed the album and put it back in the trunk. But before she did, he caught a glimpse of white satin and beads.

"What's that?"

"My wedding dress," she said, snapping the lid closed with a final click. "I had it cleaned and sent it back to

Aunt Maud, in case... I mean she paid for it and I didn't have any room to store it, so....'' He saw the pulse pound at the base of her throat. "It's not good to dwell on the past," she said bravely. "It just brings back sad memories.''

Cody regarded her with narrowed eyes. He had the feeling she wasn't only talking about her childhood. She was talking about their engagement. He wished he hadn't seen the damn dress. He didn't want to stir up any sad memories either. "Right," he said brusquely. "It's time to forget the past and move forward." He raised the trapdoor and started down the ladder. She followed close behind.

"You're not leaving, are you?" she asked, pausing on the landing at the second floor. "Without Babou?" Her voice rose and quivered.

"Look, Margaret, we've been over the whole house. He probably went outside for a breath of fresh air. I'll come over tomorrow and we'll look some more. But right now I'm tired. I've had a hard day and it's not over yet. I've got animals to feed, bills to pay, a holy mess to clean up....''

"And one lost boa constrictor to find. I tell you, Cody, I'm not sleeping in this house with Babou on the loose. Would you? The world's most macho cowboy who never cries and eats nails for breakfast? No, you wouldn't. Not even you," she said, pointing her finger at him. Her chest was rising and falling rapidly, her face was flushed and her eyes were unnaturally bright. She had worked herself into a frenzy.

"Where *will* you sleep?" he asked.

"I don't know."

He paused. "I suppose you can come home with me."

"With you?" she asked, as if he'd suggested spending the night with a serial killer.

"Then go to a hotel," he said, and stomped down the stairs to the front door. Lord, she was maddening.

She took the stairs two at a time and almost ran into him at the front door. "There is no hotel in Second Chance."

"That's right."

"In other words, get out of town," she said, glaring at him.

"This is frontier country, Margaret. There's fox and coyote and buffalo. And boa constrictors. Maybe you don't belong here."

"Don't tell me where I don't belong," she snapped.

She was so angry, he half expected steam to rise from the top of her head. Now that would be something to see... If he had time. But he didn't.

"Good night," he said, and shut the door behind him.

She'll be fine, he told himself as he drove down the highway. He'd done everything he could possibly do and it wasn't enough. It never was for Margaret. If she was scared, all she had to do was to close her bedroom door and go to bed. He'd checked her bedroom. The closet and under the bed. He frowned as he pulled into his driveway. He hadn't checked the desk drawers. He could hear her voice if he had. *Do you really think a snake could open a drawer?*

How should he know what they could do? All he knew was they had hundreds of vertebrae. Which was how they could crawl and climb and swim so fast. They liked to be warm. They couldn't swallow horses or cows, but they could swallow an animal bigger than themselves. A human? A woman?

Of course not, he said to himself as he walked into his living room and stared morosely at the dirty plates, glasses and tattered napkins. He was getting as bad as her worrying about a pet snake. He turned his back on the mess in his living room and went to his bathroom to take a shower. Then he lay down in his bed and tried to ignore the scent of roses that clung to his sheets. Squeezed his eyes shut and tried to forget the look on her face when she climaxed and the sound of her voice calling his name.

When sleep finally came, it was filled with dreams of snakes. A snake climbing the stairs, crawling into her bed, rearing its head back and swallowing her whole. And in the morning there was nothing left but feathers and hair. Sweat pouring off his face, he sat up bolt upright and gasped for air. He reached for the phone then stopped himself. It was a dream. She was asleep. Everyone was asleep but him. He was a fool to worry about her.

Margaret stood in the middle of her bedroom, chills running up and down her spine. She told herself her room was a child's room and her fears were childish. She was an adult now and more than a match for a twenty-pound snake. Even if it was hiding in her bed. She ripped the quilt and the sheets off the bed and shook them fiercely. Breathing hard, she carefully remade the bed. Then she closed the bedroom door, changed into her nightgown and crawled in between the sheets. With the lights on, she lay there watching and waiting until dawn. And thinking. Thinking she should have left immediately after the funeral. That would have saved hard feelings and harsh words and pleased Cody.

Since she hadn't left, she was stuck in the same town with him. But that didn't mean she'd have to keep running into him. As soon as he posed for the centerfold and she got his alleged friend into the magazine, there would be no reason to see him. None at all. She might go for days, weeks, months, without seeing him.

Yes. When the sun rose over the purple mountains in the east, she was filled with a new sense of purpose. She reached for the pencil and pad of paper on the nightstand and made a new list.

1. Find Babou.
2. Set up photo shoot for Cody.
3. Set up interview with mysterious friend.
4. Hide out for rest of year.
5. Forget Cody Ralston.

Five

Cody got the message on his machine the next morning. "He's back," her voice said tersely. "Come and get him." He heaved a sigh of relief. She hadn't said on his machine how she'd found the snake, but it didn't matter. As long as Babou was back.

He wasted no time in driving to her house. The front door was unlocked. Not uncommon for Second Chance. The last crime committed in town was cattle rustling in 1898.

"Margaret," he shouted. The house was eerily quiet and he felt a stab of disappointment. There was no one home but Babou, who was coiled up in the corner of his terrarium. The hole in its screen lid had been taped shut.

"Where were *you*?" Cody asked the snake as he carried the heavy glass enclosure to his truck. Instead of answering, Babou stuck his forked tongue out in Cody's direction.

"Okay, okay. So you've been neglected. Blame it on Margaret. Not me." Yes, if he thought about it, pretty much everything could be blamed on Margaret. The broken thresher, the decline of the buffalo market. But he wasn't going to think about it. He was going to stop thinking and start doing some work on the range instead of pouring over the books, trying to figure out how to pay for the skylight and the special feed for the buffalo. Then he was going to march into her office with Jake in tow, settle that matter and then hire her to remodel the bedroom. And once he got *that* matter settled, once the skylight was installed and tested, under prime conditions, he'd be through with her. For good.

When he staggered into his kitchen under the weight of the terrarium, his phone was ringing. He set the glass box on the counter and lunged for the phone.

"Did you get my message?" she asked.

"I got your message and I got your snake."

"*Your* snake."

"Whatever. Where was he?"

"He was back in his terrarium this morning. I don't know where he spent the night."

"I told you you had nothing to worry about."

"I have plenty to worry about. The first thing is your picture for the centerfold. I found Aunt Maud's photographer and set up an appointment at your place for eleven o'clock this morning. The magazine is ready to go to the printer."

"This morning?" he repeated, alarmed. "Wait a minute. I haven't had breakfast yet. I can't have my picture taken on an empty stomach."

"We'll be there at eleven o'clock," she said firmly. "Breakfast or no breakfast."

"We?"

"This is important. Our first centerfold. I want to make

sure he gets the right angle and that you're dressed properly."

"I thought clothing was optional."

"I...I... Is that what she said?"

"Do you want to check the will?"

"No, I don't. I'm in charge now and I'm not going to be in charge of a sleazy magazine."

"If I'm too sleazy, maybe you should find someone else."

"Maybe you should find some other magazine for your friend."

He glared at the telephone. "You win. I'll be dressed at eleven o'clock."

"In clean jeans," she said.

"That's all?" he asked.

"Along with your usual underwear," she said casually. A little too casually.

"Is my usual underwear good enough for a national magazine?" he asked, watching Babou coil himself around the tree stump in his terrarium.

"No one's going to see it," she said.

"Then why bother?"

There was such a long silence, he was afraid she'd hung up. "Then don't wear any underwear," she said in an exasperated voice. "I don't care."

"What about the readers?"

"They won't know. Until they start arriving by the busload, and camping out on your doorstep."

"Would that bother you?" he asked.

"As long as they buy the magazine, I'll be delighted," she assured him.

"What if they throw themselves at me, and rip my clothes off for souvenirs?" The picture wasn't altogether displeasing. Especially the effect it would have on Margaret. He could just see her turning green with jealousy.

"This seems to be a recurring fantasy of yours," she said. "It's getting late. Go eat breakfast."

"My usual bowl of nails."

"I don't have time to joke around," she said impatiently.

"Too bad. Your aunt did."

"I'm tired of being compared to her. I'm tired of your criticizing me and I'm tired—I'm just tired. I didn't sleep very well last night...." Her voice drifted off until he could barely hear the last words, and he felt a wave of sympathy for her. Which was pointless. She had no sympathy for him. And he hadn't slept well last night, either.

He had a vision of dark circles under her eyes, her eyelashes fluttering and closing. "Go back to bed," he ordered. "The world will keep turning without you." And the photo shoot could go on without her, too.

Margaret didn't answer. The line went dead and he hung up. Maybe she'd fallen asleep on her feet. If he was there, he'd carry her upstairs and put her to bed. Let her catch a few more z's. In that frilly, girlish room he remembered so well. Under the canopy, between the flowered sheets. He buried his head in his hands, tormented himself by thinking of the things they could do there. If he was there. If he wasn't so tired. If she wasn't mad at him for not finding Babou. If she didn't think he was sleazy. He groaned aloud.

"Boss?"

He jerked his head up and looked into the bleary eyes of his foreman. "Thank God, you're up," Cody said, gripping him by both shoulders. "Don't go anywhere. That was Margaret on the phone. She'll be here at eleven o'clock. You can meet her. You feeling okay?"

Jake nodded, then glanced down at the contents of the terrarium. His eyes widened. "Thought I was better. But

when I start seeing snakes, it's time to go back to bed."
Shaking his head, he turned on his heel and left the room.

"No, wait," Cody called, but he'd gone.

Margaret arrived at the ranch fifteen minutes early to
meet Chuck the photographer in front of the farmhouse.

"I don't know…" Chuck said, unloading his equip-
ment from the back of his van. "Your aunt always had
the pictures taken in the studio."

Margaret sighed. Would they ever stop comparing her
to her aunt? Would she ever be judged on her own, for
who she was? "I know," she said. "But I'm going for a
different approach. A more earthy look."

"Plenty of earth around here," he admitted, glancing
at the green fields that stretched as far as the horizon.

"What I have in mind," she said as she walked around
the house, staggering under the weight of Chuck's camera
case, "is something out by the barn. A haystack for example. We'll get the whole thing set up and lit before he
ever knows we're here. Then we pose him on the hay,
you take the picture and we're out of here."

"Sounds simple," Chuck said.

Margaret nodded. But a gnawing feeling in her stomach
told her nothing involving Cody was ever simple. So far,
though, everything was going like clockwork. They found
the perfect bale of hay, dragged it to a sunny spot in front
of the barn. Chuck set up the lights, reflectors, his tripod
and camera and had Margaret pose so he could set his
lights.

She slipped out of her high heels and reclined along
the length of the bale in her slim navy skirt and cotton
knit shirt.

"Head up," Chuck instructed. "Eyes over here. Shoulders turned to the left."

"Whoa," Cody said, barreling around the corner of the

barn and stopping suddenly. "Look at Ms. Centerfold. Put yourself in the magazine and I guarantee you'll find somebody to marry."

Margaret sat up straight and smoothed her skirt over her knees. "I'm not looking for somebody to marry."

"I thought that was one of the conditions of the will. 'Concerted effort to find a husband,'" he said.

"Thanks for reminding me," she said.

"My pleasure," he drawled. "And if you ask me—" he ambled over, took her hand and helped her down from her perch on the haystack "—it won't be easy to find somebody to meet your high standards."

"I didn't ask you." The touch of his callused palm sent shock waves traveling up her arm and straight to the core of her being. She didn't want his opinion. Or his constant criticism. She didn't want anything from him except to get over him. As it was, she couldn't touch him without feeling she was caught in a Rocky Mountain avalanche. Or look at him without mentally undressing him. Without wanting to make love to him. She had to get over him. And she would. Any day now.

She was just checking him out. That's all. Clean jeans, yes. Hair uncombed. What did she expect? He could cover it with his hat. Flannel shirt, unbuttoned. Had to come off.

"Chuck, you know Cody, don't you?"

"Yep."

"Shall we get started?" she asked.

Cody shrugged. "You're the boss."

She gave him a sharp glance. Since when was she the boss when he was around? Since when had he ever done anything she said? "Okay. Take your shirt off and put your hat on," she instructed. "And assume the same position you saw me in."

He did what she said, then propped his elbow in the hay, stuck a straw between his teeth and gave the camera a sexy grin. Oh, Lord, the look on his face. The hair on his chest glinting in the morning sun, tapering down to the low-cut Levi's. Her mouth went dry as the air off the great plains as she wondered if he'd taken her advice and worn his everyday boxers or nothing at all.

She paced restlessly in back of the camera as Chuck yelled to him.

"Look left. Look right. Straight ahead. Head down. Chin up."

He did it all without dropping the smile or the hay in his teeth. And then it was over. His hair curled damply over his forehead from the heat of Chuck's lights. He slung his shirt over one suntanned shoulder, and mopped his brow, and Margaret found herself short of breath. Probably from all that pacing she'd been doing.

"How's your friend today?" she asked as Cody walked her to her car. She couldn't resist sliding glances in his direction. Who could resist feasting their eyes on all six-foot-three inches of bare-chested man? He carried the camera case as if it weighed no more than a piece of straw and loaded it into Chuck's van before he pulled away.

"Better. Much better."

"I suppose he made a miraculous recovery after I left."

"Yes, he did, but he had a relapse when he saw Babou today."

"That's understandable. Tell him I'm looking forward to meeting him. Tell him if it's not today I won't be able to squeeze him into the May issue. I'm already working on June with a feature called Bad Boys from the Badlands. How do you like it?"

"Bad Boys from the Badlands," he repeated. "That was your idea or one your aunt left behind?"

"It's mine. Is it so hard to believe that I might have an idea or two of my own? That I might want to put my own mark on the magazine?"

He stifled a grin that annoyed her. "Not at all. I just remember it wasn't that long ago you were taking over the magazine to fulfill a promise, to keep it in the family and all that. Now you're putting your mark on it. What next?"

"Next I have to find some bad boys for the issue. What do you think? Will I be able to find any bad boys? Besides you, that is." It was absurd how much she wanted his approval. How quickly she'd forgotten how he'd left her alone in the house with a snake overnight. And how much she wanted to show him and her aunt—wherever she was—that she could make a go of the magazine, maybe even boost circulation, with new features.

"You think I'm bad?" he asked, trapping her against the side of the car with his arms.

She felt the heat radiate from his body. The heady masculine scent of his hair and skin threatened to overwhelm her. Her knees buckled. Her throat was so tight she couldn't speak. In answer to his question, she shrugged.

She should have known he'd take it as a personal challenge. With the noonday sun beating down on his head, and a hundred or more buffalo watching them curiously from behind their white fence, he put his broad palms on her hips and lifted her onto the hood of the Bronco. Her skirt rode up to her thighs. She gasped. The metal was smooth and warm against her bare skin. She ran her hands down the muscles of his chest, through the dusting of dark curls, then lower...

Cody yanked her off the hood of the truck and dragged her up against his throbbing masculinity. Then he took her mouth in a hard, hot, furious kiss. He had that look in his eyes, that fierce possessive look she recognized. She saw what was going to happen next. She waited for it. Wanted it. Ached for it. But she couldn't have it. Not now. Not in the middle of the day, in the middle of the ranch. She gripped his arms so tightly, she must have cut off his circulation, and he pulled away.

"I'm sorry," she said under her breath.

"You're sorry. What else is new?"

"Look, Cody…"

"No, you look. You can't turn hot and cold. Off and on. You can't come back here and take up where you left off. You've got to pay your dues first, sweetheart. And you've got to follow through and finish what you start."

"What…what do you mean?"

"You can start by reinstating Ladies' Night at the saloon. The boys miss it."

"Okay, fine."

"And then you can put that skylight in."

"I'll send a carpenter."

"Not for the test you won't."

"You mean…"

"That's exactly what I mean."

She bit her lower lip. The smoldering look in his eyes made her tingle with anticipation. If he knew how much she wanted him. Wanted him then and wanted him now. The pungent smell of hay in the air brought back memories. Of yesterday and so many other yesterdays. But what about tomorrow? Would there be a future for them? Afraid to hope, afraid to love, afraid to say anything else, she staggered backward, got into her car and drove away.

Back at the office she looked at her list. Proudly she checked off the first two items. She'd found Babou, or rather *he'd* found his way back home. She'd done the photo shoot and avoided any disastrous results, but she hadn't set up an appointment with Cody's friend. As for hiding out for the rest of the year, that didn't look possible anymore.

Cody was right. She was sending mixed signals to him. Hot and cold. Off and on. From now on she would be cold and off. If she started something, she would finish it. As for testing his skylight, that was so far in the future, she wouldn't worry about it. Which didn't mean she wouldn't think about it. The idea of making love with him while the rain danced off the skylight, while lightning streaked across the sky and thunder drowned out the sound of their cries made her blood heat up. With a sigh she crossed off the last item on her list. Forgetting Cody was too difficult at this time.

Her eyes closed and she let her head sink down on a pile of papers. She told herself she'd done enough for one day. She was too tired to accomplish another thing. On the other hand, there was so much to be done before she went to the printer tomorrow. Instead of allowing herself to drift into a much-needed sleep with her cheek on a stack of bills, she put her braided Chanel jacket on and went out to get a cup of coffee at the diner, where Maud had found a second home, eating dinner most nights and conducting business over coffee in the back booth.

Avoiding the back booth, Margaret chose the third from the door. "Just coffee, Dorothy," she said when the middle-aged waitress approached.

"Okay, hon. Cream and sugar just like your aunt?" she asked.

"Black."

"Piece of cherry pie? Hot out of the oven."

"No thanks." Margaret stared out the window without seeing the dry goods store or the feed and fuel. If she didn't get that coffee soon, her brain would cease to function. When a man pressed his craggy, weather-beaten face against the window outside her booth, she was so startled, she jumped.

The eyes that stared in at her were blue and bleary. He was tall, about Cody's height. A few minutes later, he came in and sat opposite her in the booth.

"Ms. Margaret," he said, removing his hat. "I'm Jake Rasmussen, from out at the Ralston ranch."

The mystery man. Cody's foreman. "Of course, I remember. How are you?"

"Pretty fair. Well, not so good, to tell the truth. But Cody said I got to get ahold of you if I want to get into the magazine."

"Yes. Fine," she said, taking a pencil from her purse and reaching for a paper napkin. "You're looking for a wife, then."

His high cheekbones turned bright red. "Not me—a friend."

Margaret cleared her throat. Where had she heard this before? Maybe no self-respecting man would ever admit that he couldn't find a woman on his own. "I wonder if it's the same friend Cody was telling me about."

"Could be," he said, reaching into his shirt pocket. "I brought in a picture like he told me to do."

Margaret held it up to the light from the window. The man in the picture could have been anybody. Any cowboy, that is. His face was shaded by his hat and he was standing twenty yards from the camera next to a horse. "This is you?" she asked. "I mean your friend?"

"Right. Do you think he's got a chance?"

"Yes, of course. Women love cowboys," she assured him.

"That's what Cody said."

"He would know," she said dryly. "What would you—your friend, I mean—like to say in the ad?" she asked.

Jake hesitated, rubbing his chin with his hand while Dorothy set two cups of coffee on the table. "Got any pie?" he asked the waitress.

She nodded, went into the kitchen and came back with a piece.

"Would he be looking for someone to pluck chickens, bake biscuits and keep him company on long winter nights?" Margaret prodded gently.

Jake drew his scraggly eyebrows together. "He used to be, when he was young. But he knows better now. See, he's been disappointed in love once. 'Bout broke his heart. So he's willing to settle for less."

Margaret stared at him. Was he talking about himself, a friend, or was he talking about Cody? "In this case, less might be more," she said, thoughtfully tapping her pencil on the table. "I mean, he might find a different kind of woman he liked even better, even though she wasn't interested in baking or plucking."

"What kind?" he asked.

"Well, someone who's independent and strong-minded, but who's tired of the rat race and city slickers. Who's looking for a simpler way of life and who wants a man who means what he says."

"Is that what *you* want?" he asked.

Margaret gazed over his head, out the window to the street and the mountains in the distance. What *did* she want? Though she claimed to miss the city and the opportunity she had to succeed there, wasn't there something somewhere deep inside her that longed to return to her roots? Could she deny that men like Cody were more virile, more sexy, more exciting than anyone she'd met in Chicago? She had to admit Cody always meant what he said. Sometimes she wished he didn't.

"I have everything I want," she assured him, watching him eat his pie.

When he finished, he looked up. "You're a good artist, you know. The picture you did of Cody, the one you gave him for his birthday, looks just like him."

She flushed with pleasure at the compliment. "Oh, you saw it?"

"I see it every time I go into the bunkhouse. Me and the boys pinned a copy to the dart board."

Her face fell.

"Just for fun," he explained. "We don't mean no disrespect."

"No, of course not." She took a deep breath and smiled encouragingly. "Now, tell me a little bit more about your friend so we can round out the profile. So far, all I know is that he was once brokenhearted. Is he—did he ever get over it?"

Jake set his fork down. "Says he did, but I don't think so. Not the way he's acting lately. Like a lovesick bull."

"I didn't know bulls got lovesick. I thought they operated on instinct. Or hormones." Like Cody.

Jake went on to say the man he was talking about lived on a ranch, rode horses and played the harmonica. Which meant he could be almost anyone. Except for the harmonica, he could even be Cody.

"Does your friend know you're putting him in the magazine?"

Jake shook his head violently. "He wouldn't like it. Says he don't need nobody. But I don't believe him. Everybody needs somebody. Ain't that true?" His blue eyes pierced hers.

"What about you?" she asked before he could ask her the same thing. But he never got to answer. At that moment, Cody breezed into the diner.

"Mind if I join you?" he asked, and without waiting for an answer, he sat down next to Margaret, pressing his thigh against hers. She tensed. The shock waves rippled through her body and straight to the core. She moved toward the wall, but he moved with her, shoulder to shoulder, hip to hip.

"We're having a business meeting," she informed him.

"Thought so. How's the pie?" he asked Jake.

"Can't recommend it highly enough," Jake said.

Cody signaled Dorothy and ordered himself a cup of coffee and pie for both him and Margaret.

"No thanks," she said.

He turned his face in her direction, so close, she was forced to look at him. "You gotta eat something. You look like you're going to blow away. Dorothy," he called, "bring her a bowl of soup, too."

"Since when are you in charge of feeding me?" she demanded.

"Since I saw you chowing down at my party. Realized then it was up to me. Didn't I say she looked thin, Jake?"

"Said you thought she was just as beautiful as ever."

Cody glared at Jake and Margaret smothered a smile.

"Jake here was telling me about a friend who wants to take out an ad," she said to ease the tension. She held up the picture.

Cody squinted at it. "Why that's…that's…him all right."

"Margaret says he's got a good chance. Says all women love cowboys."

"Really? That include her?" Cody asked, his blue gaze dropping to the curve of her breasts under her pale pink cotton blouse. She felt her nipples harden under his bold stare. And she knew that his sharp eyes didn't miss the response he was looking for.

"She says what women want," Jake continued, "is a more simpler life and a man who means what he says."

"That's all? Hell, we got it made, right?" Cody said with an insolent grin.

"I thought neither of you were looking for a wife," Margaret said, edging away from Cody as Dorothy set a bowl of homemade vegetable soup and a pile of crackers in front of her.

"We're not," Cody said emphatically. "But maybe

we'll change our minds when the letters start coming in, who knows?'' Cody said.

They continued to joke about marriage and women while Margaret ate her soup, and then her pie, surprised at how hungry she really was. The real affection between the two men was obvious by their lighthearted teasing. Occasionally Cody gave her a lustful look that told her more than words could that there was unfinished business between them. That he hadn't forgotten what happened this morning and what was going to happen in the future. Then he'd return to joking with Jake. Margaret was almost jealous of their camaraderie. It was clear they'd do anything for each other. Even advertise for a wife? She wondered.

''Do you play the harmonica, Cody?'' she asked during a pause in the conversation.

''Sure. Why, do women want music, too?'' he asked with a sexy grin.

''Some do. Some don't. I just wondered.''

Cody asked for the check and laid his money on the table. When she tried to pay, he stopped her by squeezing her hand in his larger one. The warmth and strength of his grip made the fires of passion flare to life once again. Damn him. If he didn't want her around, if he wanted to see her leave town, why did he touch her like that? Why did he tease her? She was so tired today and so vulnerable, it was all she could do to pull her hand away and stand up.

''Okay,'' she said, looking down at the generous tip he'd left on the table. ''But I owe you a meal.''

''Two meals. Don't forget the barbecue. And that's not all,'' he said meaningfully.

She turned and walked out of the diner, her cheeks flaming, her head held high, and went directly home. She didn't even make it up the stairs to her bedroom. She crashed on the futon in the solarium and slept for ten hours.

Cody didn't see Margaret for the next week. He communicated with her by leaving messages on her machine. She responded in kind. The messages concerned the skylight and Ladies' Night. In her usual organized fashion she'd arranged for both. In fact, a carpenter was already at work sawing a hole in his roof while he was back in his office making calls, trying to sell his buffalo. At least it kept his mind off Margaret. Somewhat.

His goal was still to make love with Margaret under the skylight in a blinding rainstorm. Where the raging elements outside matched the raging passion inside. To drive her out of his mind once and for all. He still believed it could be done. Although there were times—like when he saw her in baggy sweats the night in her attic, pictured her posing on that bale of hay, her skirt halfway up her thigh or watched her eat soup—he wondered if he could do it. Walk out on her after he'd made love to her.

Of course he could. He remembered the pain. Relived his anger. She'd done it to him. He could do it to her. He wanted her to know how it felt. He wanted her to suffer as much as he had.

He wouldn't see her until Tuesday, Ladies' Night at the saloon. He wouldn't be going if he hadn't nagged her so much about it. He even had second thoughts as he and Jake were driving into town Tuesday night.

"Think Margaret knows it's me who wants a wife?" Jake asked.

"Doubt it. Not from the picture you gave her. I think she thinks it's me."

"Why would you advertise in *Lonesome Cowboy*? You're young, good-lookin'...."

"Margaret doesn't think so."

"Sure she does. I seen her lookin' at you like a lovesick calf."

"A lovesick calf, huh?" Cody chuckled mirthlessly. "That'll be the day."

"What's keepin' you two lovebirds apart?" Jake asked.

"Calves, lovebirds... Don't forget the bees and the rabbits and the squirrels. You've got some imagination, old buddy."

"You'll see," Jake said calmly. "You don't really think she's too thin, do you?"

"I'm not going to tell you what I think because you've got a loose tongue. 'Just as beautiful as ever.' That was between you and me. I can't believe I really said that."

"Maybe you didn't say it, but you thought it. That day you came back from the funeral."

"Even if I did, you've got no right to read my mind and repeat my thoughts. Do *you* think she's still beautiful?" Cody asked casually.

"Purty as a picture."

"A picture of Benedict Arnold."

Jake shook his head. "'Bout time you forgot about the past and thought about the future."

"There's no future for Margaret and me," Cody said gruffly as they pulled up in front of the saloon.

The place was packed. More crowded than Maud's funeral celebration—and louder. And Margaret was having a fine old time. He could tell by the flush that tinted her cheeks, by the way she was surrounded by cowboys, laughing merrily at whatever they said and taking notes on her ever-present clipboard. Her silvery laughter carried across the room and filled him with bitter longing. She wasn't his anymore. He didn't expect her to spend any time with him. She was there to scare up business. But was there a law against saying hello at least? Apparently so, he thought as he stared gloomily around the room.

When he could no longer stand watching her bat her eyelashes at every man in the room, he pushed his way through the crowd and took her firmly by the arm. "Can I talk to you for a minute?"

"I'm kind of busy," she said with a smile for the three men she'd been talking to. But none for him.

"I can see that. But this is business."

"Oh, well in that case, go ahead."

"Can we go someplace where it's quiet?"

She wrinkled her nose, the way she did when she was annoyed.

"Outside," he said.

With Margaret in tow, he pushed his way back through the wall-to-wall bodies and out the door into the cool night air. What a relief after the smoke and the noise. She crossed her arms over her chest and tapped her foot impatiently on the raised wooden sidewalk.

"Well?"

"When am I going to get my fifty thousand dollars?"

"Anytime. Just go see Clifford. I'll let him know you fulfilled your part of the bargain. What are you going to do with it?" she asked.

"I might take a Caribbean cruise or buy a sports car," he joked, leaning against the door of the saloon. "What do you think?"

She tilted her head and studied him. The yellow beams from the old-fashioned streetlight turned her hair to ebony, her eyes became deep fathomless pools. "Take a cruise," she said finally. "You look tired."

"I am tired. I can't sleep because my bedroom's all torn up."

"How is it coming along?"

"Come out and see."

"I'm too busy. It's a lot of work running a magazine."

She brushed her hand across her forehead. "I'm tired, too."

"Why don't you take a cruise with me?"

"A cruise with you?" She shook her head in exasperation. "Talk about mixed messages. You say I'm unfit for life on the frontier, you say I can't compare to Aunt Maud. You tell me I'm too thin, and then you suggest a cruise with you? No thanks."

He shrugged. "Then I'll buy a thresher with the money and pay some bills. You haven't billed me for the skylight yet. Or asked me over for dinner."

She sighed. "I'm going to be here for a while. We have plenty of time."

"Yeah, well, like you said, I'm not getting any younger. And neither are you."

"So now I'm too old for you. Is there anything about me you like, Cody?" she asked, her chin raised a defiant notch.

She should have known better than to ask that question. She should have realized he couldn't pass up a challenge like that. He had to show her. He closed the distance between them in a flash and roughly took her mouth with his. She resisted for one brief moment. Then her lips became soft and pliant under his. With one hand tangled in her dark silky hair, he bent her head back and arched her body into his. Time and time again he brought her mouth back to his for another breathless kiss.

"I like that," he muttered. "I like your mouth. I like the way you taste. I like the way you smell." He buried his face in her hair and inhaled deeply.

She was trembling and she couldn't stop. Her head was light and her body was heavy with desire. The only thing to do was wrap her arms around him and cling for dear life. Either that or fall down. Where was her resistance? Gone the minute he touched her. She told herself he *didn't* like her. He only wanted her. Wanted to pay her back for what she'd done to him. He was trying to drive her crazy. And dear heaven, he knew how to do it. Only he knew how to make her crazy with want and need and throbbing desire.

He trailed his lips from her mouth to the sensitive spot behind her ear. To the indentation of her throat where her pulse beat fast. With his strong hands he cupped her bottom and thrust his arousal against the juncture of her thighs. Where he knew under her silk dress, under her lace bikini briefs she would be warm, wet and welcoming. And if they weren't standing on a sidewalk under a street-light... If the whole town wasn't inside the bar waiting...

"Any more questions?" he asked in a guttural growl, his lips pressed against her ear.

With trembling hands, she pushed him away, shook her head and walked unsteadily back into the saloon.

Six

Weeks went by. Weeks during which Margaret avoided the diner, the saloon and any place else she would be likely to run into Cody. For her own sanity she kept to the house and the office. He didn't call her and she didn't call him. The carpenter told her the work was done and she sent him a check. She'd collect from Cody later.

The days blended into each other, filled with proofreading, layouts and design. She worked hard all day and into the night, taking a bulging briefcase home with her most evenings. One day stood out from the others. The day the magazine hit the stands. The day it arrived into thousands of homes across America, where thousands of eager hands would rip off the brown wrapper and turn to the centerfold. They'd see him in glorious color—his bronzed skin, his blue eyes and his dark hair—every sexy inch of him, spread out for them to dream about, fantasize over and write to.

She'd seen the proofs, of course. She knew it was a good picture. But seeing it on glossy paper sent a tremor of desire through her body. Mixed emotions whirled around in her mind and confused her. She was proud of the magazine. Proud of what she'd done, featuring so-called bad boys. But she was jealous, too. Jealous of all those women who were falling for Cody as she had. And she was not proud of being jealous.

She ran her fingers over the picture, imagined she could feel the rough shadow of a beard on his jaw. She traced the breadth of his shoulders, imagining the heat from his body scorching her fingers. She looked with longing at the hair on his chest, soft and crisp to the touch. And the low-slung jeans he wore left little to the imagination. Her heart thudded loudly in her ears. Margaret turned the page quickly. There was no need to stare at it. She knew what he looked like.

Handsome devil, isn't he? Aunt Maud would have said. *But hardly marriage material. Not for you.* As if Margaret didn't know. Now, more than ever. After she'd had a taste of city life, how could she ever be happy on a ranch?

"It doesn't matter," she said as if her aunt were in the room with her. "Cody doesn't want to get married. He's only doing this to please you and to boost circulation. You know that."

What about you? came her aunt's familiar voice in her head, nagging and persistent.

"I know, you want me to look for a husband, but...but..."

You're still in love with him, aren't you? her aunt chided.

"No!" Her voice reverberated off the walls of the office and startled the mailman who was pushing the mail through the slot in the door. She had to get out of there before she went crazy. Talking to a dead woman. Losing her cool over a picture in a magazine. It was time to renew old acquaintances. To expand her small circle of friends. To join one of Aunt Maud's clubs. Maybe all of them. It would take her mind off Cody. She'd start with the bridge club. Next Monday. No chance of running into him there.

She didn't run into him at the bridge club, but she was forced to listen to everyone talk about him. Sitting across the table from Helen Dorsey, holding a handful of cards and nibbling on cashew nuts, Margaret couldn't escape the barrage of questions about her ex-fiancé or the image of him sprawled across the page in the magazine, a staple in his navel. It was right there on Helen's coffee table, open to the centerfold. Just in case anyone had missed it. No one had.

"How in the world did you ever get him to pose for you?" Mary Lynn Barnard asked, leaning forward in her chair and putting her elbows on the table.

"It was Aunt Maud who asked him. In her will. He felt he couldn't refuse a deathbed wish," Margaret explained, sorting her cards.

"As if he needed to advertise for a woman." Lydia Graham snorted behind her cards.

"That's what Cody said," Margaret said. "Is he really that popular?"

Helen raised her eyebrows over the ornate frames of her glasses. "Oh my, yes. He's quite the playboy. Or was. I hear he's all business these days."

"Really?" Margaret took a sip of frosty homemade lemonade.

"You know, he's saddled with all those buffalo. Will says it's the stupidest thing he's ever heard. Raising buffalo. But that's Cody. Always trying something new. Whether it's women or livestock."

Margaret felt her cheeks redden as she pictured the hordes of women parading through his bedroom. Seduced by Cody on the same bed she'd made love to him on. Six years ago. And more recently. She pushed the disturbing thoughts out of her mind. "I understand buffalo is actually leaner than beef and better for you," she said.

"Listen to her," Lydia teased. "A regular member of the Buffalo Advisory Board."

"Not me," Margaret protested. "All I know is that I tried it and I thought it was delicious. That's all."

"Margaret," Helen said, tapping her cards on the table. "It's your bid."

"Oh, sorry. One heart."

"So, what's the story with you and Cody?" Mary Lynn asked, looking at Margaret over her cards.

"No story," Margaret said firmly. "It's over between us."

"That's not what I heard. I heard you two disappeared for a long time at Cody's birthday party. What were you doing, a taste test?" She giggled.

Margaret stared at the cards in front of her face without seeing them. "We were discussing some remodeling he wants done at the ranch. In fact, he had a skylight put in...in..." She couldn't bring herself to say the word *bedroom*. "In his house."

"Someone saw you two at the diner," Helen remarked. "Acting very cozy."

"That was business. We were talking about his ad in the magazine."

"Good picture of Cody," Lydia chimed in. "But I thought those centerfolds were usually in the nude, not that I read that kind of magazine, of course."

"There are magazines that do that. But *Lonesome Cowboy* is not one of them," Margaret said primly.

"Maybe you didn't want anyone else but you to see your fiancé in the buff," Mary Lynn suggested.

"Mary Lynn," Helen said in a shocked voice. "Margaret is over Cody. That's what you said. Didn't you, dear?''

Margaret forced a polite smile and nodded. She should never have come. She hated bridge and she hated talking about Cody. She'd come to get away from him, but that was all these women could talk about. It was time to change the subject.

''Beautiful spring weather,'' she said.

''I hear we're going to get some rain,'' Lydia said.

''Rain?'' In disbelief Margaret glanced out the window at the few puffy clouds in the bright blue sky. ''It doesn't look like rain.'' It couldn't rain. She hoped Cody had forgotten about testing his new skylight with her in the rain but maybe he hadn't. He usually didn't forget things like that. The idea had caused her many sleepless nights. Nights when she prayed for a yearlong drought.

''You never know around here,'' Mary Lynn said. ''The weather's as unpredictable as the people. Take you, Margaret. We thought you were gone for good. Maud said you'd probably marry some city slicker and never come back. But here you are, back again. Going on twenty-six and still not married.'' She paused and all three ladies gave Margaret faintly curious looks over their cards. As if they were looking for some fatal flaw to explain her alleged spinsterhood, like a nervous tic or shingles.

''I was busy working,'' she explained. ''With no time to socialize.''

''Let that be a lesson to you,'' Helen said. ''And don't make that mistake again. You're not getting any younger. Now's your chance to meet some real men. We've got plenty to choose from in the valley. If Cody's not good enough for you.''

''It's not that. In fact, Cody's made it clear that I'm not good enough for him.''

''He said that?'' Lydia asked in a shocked voice.

Helen shook her head. "Isn't that just like him? Takes after the Mountcastles, his mother's people. Good-looking, high-spirited, prickly as cactus. But loyal."

"Loyal!" As soon as she'd left town she heard Cody had lost no time in taking up with other women. Not that she blamed him.

"Yes, even last year, in the dead of winter, when there was no work, he kept the whole crew on full pay. They'd do anything for him and vice versa."

Which explained why Cody was so anxious to get Jake's advertisement into the magazine. He'd do anything to help him find a wife. Yes, loyalty was a good thing. Too bad it didn't extend to her. But she didn't deserve his loyalty, she reminded herself. And she didn't want it. All she wanted was to get through the year and leave town without getting hurt.

"So," Helen interjected, "what's going to happen when all the women in America write to Cody and propose to him? Are you ready for that, Margaret?"

"Of course," she said blithely. "It will be great for circulation."

"But is Cody ready?" Mary Lynn inquired. "I thought he was having too much fun to get married."

Helen stood to refill the glasses. "That's what men always say. Until they're ready. Really ready. Then it doesn't matter who she is. If she comes along at the right time, the man will marry her."

Margaret's cards were sticking to her hands. She had no idea what the bid was or whose turn it was. She wondered if every meeting turned into a gossip session. Just when she thought she'd go crazy if she had to stay there another minute, the telephone rang and it was the post-mistress calling to ask Margaret to come by the post office with her truck to pick up her mail. How she knew where

Margaret was was one of those mysteries of small-town life.

The women bubbled over with excitement. The cards were left forgotten on the table while Margaret put her jacket on and found her car keys.

"I told you," Helen said. "I told you every woman in America would write to him. Now what's he going to do? How's he ever going to choose just one?"

"He'll have interviews. He'll ask for pictures or videos. That's the latest thing," Lydia explained.

"Or maybe they'll have to write an essay on why they want to be married to Cody," Mary Lynn suggested. "As if he didn't know. After seeing that picture, I almost wrote in myself."

"You didn't! What would Carl say?" Lydia asked.

"I'm kidding. Don't tell me you weren't tempted?"

"Or how about this?" Helen said. "Have them send a sample of their buttermilk biscuits. The way to a man's heart..."

Margaret stood at the front door, listening to them as they fueled each other's excitement. She wanted to laugh and she wanted to cry. Most of all, she wanted to leave. But she couldn't do either for fear of hurting their feelings. When they finally let her go, it was with the understanding that she'd tell them exactly what was in all those letters.

The air in Cody's kitchen was thick with smoke and filled with raucous laughter. "Hey, dude, I'll raise you two and see your aces," Cody's friend Harris called across the kitchen table. When the phone rang, Cody put his cards facedown on the table, reached for the portable phone with one hand, held his cigar in the other and barked hello.

"Cody? I can hardly hear you."

"Same here. Speak up."

"I have some letters for you,"

"It's the post office," he explained to his friends. "They got some mail for me."

"The post office closed two hours ago," she explained patiently. "This is Margaret. Can you come to my office and pick up your mail?"

He took a puff on his cigar. "No can do, Margaret. Not with a straight flush in my hands."

Howls of anguish greeted this remark, followed by more laughter. Followed by the sound of Margaret hanging up.

"So what'd she say?" Jesse Franklin asked, holding his cards against his chest. "She wants you back?"

"Yeah. But I told her I was busy. You heard me," Cody told his friend the sheriff.

"Hasn't changed that much," Harris remarked. "Still good-looking."

"Still stubborn, pigheaded, unreasonable, obstinate..." Cody added.

"Sounds like you still got it bad," Harris said with a knowing grin.

"What about it? You going to give her another chance?" Bart asked.

"No deal," Cody assured him. "Margaret and I are history."

"You sure? I saw the way you were looking at her at your party," Jesse said. "Like you were hungry."

"I *was* hungry. Didn't have time to eat. You don't think I'd take her back after what she did to me?" Cody asked incredulously. "Would you?"

"If she came crawling on her knees," Jesse told Cody.

"Margaret on her knees? Ha!" That would be the day. Still the idea had some merit.

"You'll find somebody else to marry," Will assured him.

"I don't want somebody else. I don't want to get married."

"Then why advertise in *Lonesome Cowboy?*"

"I told you. It was Muddy's last request. I couldn't turn her down."

As Cody picked up his cards and deliberately reshuffled them, Will Dorsey surveyed him through narrowed eyes. "Helen says Margaret was touting your buffalo at bridge. Said it was leaner than beef and better for you. Said it was delicious. How much you have to pay her to say that?"

"I don't have to pay her. It's the truth." Cody frowned. "I didn't know she played bridge."

"Not very well, Helen says. Maybe because she couldn't keep her mind on the cards. Helen thinks she's still got it bad for you. Why else would she say that about buffalo?"

"Why? Because it's true. Admit it. You guys are just jealous. Because I had the smarts to buy buffalo first." He paused. He didn't want to ask, but he had to know. "What else did she say?"

"Said she was doing some remodeling for you."

"That's right. It's done." All but the testing. He was waiting for a rainy night for that. He was waiting with heart-pounding impatience. He'd been waiting since the last nail was pounded into the skylight. He'd been watching the weather reports, listening to the long-range forecast. Waiting for the rain, the storm, the power outage. Candles would flicker on his dresser, turning her skin to amber, her hair to ebony. After they made love until they couldn't move—until they were drained, exhausted and completely sated—then he'd truthfully be able to say he and Margaret were history.

He tilted his chair back and propped his boots on the table. The faces around the table receded, the voices faded. All he could see was Margaret's face, her eyes blazing with passion. All he could hear was her voice, whispering his name in his ear. Was it possible she still cared about him, he wondered. Hope flickered like the wings of a moth. Until he squashed it.

"Hey, Cody. Where were you? Let's see your hand."

His chair came crashing down onto the old linoleum and with it, his fantasy. They played a few more hands, paid off the winners and the crowd dispersed, standing out in front of the house in the clear night air trading insults.

"So, what're the odds of you and Margaret hooking up again?" Jesse asked Cody from the driveway.

"Zero," Cody retorted.

"I got even money says you're wrong."

"What? Is my love life open to bets?" Cody demanded, looking around openmouthed at his circle of friends.

"Why not?" Will asked with a chuckle. "We all got money on it. You want in?"

"Me, bet against me and Margaret getting back together? That's like taking candy from a baby," Cody said.

"Go ahead, then, if you're so sure."

"Put up or shut up."

"One hundred dollars says we're through," Cody said.

"You're on," Will said, taking a notepad out of his back pocket.

When Margaret drove up in the Bronco, the men headed for their cars. "We know when we're not wanted," Harris said loudly. "Why didn't you tell us you had a late date?"

"Don't leave on my account," Margaret told Cody's friends. "I'm delivering Cody's mail, that's all."

"At this time of night? How does he rate?" Bart asked.

"By being *Lonesome Cowboy*'s first centerfold. What about it? Who wants to sign up for next month? We've got a special going. Guaranteed results or your money back."

"First we want to see what happens to Cody," Bart said with a pointed glance at his friend. "We're all waiting."

"Yeah, we're betting things will turn out good, aren't we, Cody?"

Cody shook his head, ignoring them as well as Margaret's puzzled glance.

After they were gone, Margaret stood next to her car, looking up at the sky as if she'd forgotten about him, his friends, the mail and everything else. Cody leaned against his front door, drinking in the sight of her. Wondering if the bet was such a sure thing, after all. He hadn't seen her for days, no weeks. He'd gone these six years without seeing her, with no trouble. Not much anyway. So how did it happen now that a day without Margaret was like a day without sunshine or coffee or air?

In the porch light her face was sculpted of marble, her hair a dark cloud. Restless, unable to stay away from her, he crossed the driveway and leaned on the car, pressing his shoulder against hers, absorbing the warmth from her body, inhaling the scent of roses that he'd come to associate with her. It wasn't enough. He needed to get closer. To taste and plunder her mouth. Tangle his hands in her hair. Hold her prisoner in his arms.

He clenched his hands into fists. If she had it "bad" for him, wouldn't he know it? Wouldn't she look at him instead of the sky? Turn toward him, so he could see the rise and fall of her breasts under her cotton sweater? Tilt her face up to his, look into his eyes so he could see the banked fires of passion that matched his own? Give him a sign? But she didn't look at him. She watched the clouds obscure the Big Dipper and the North Star. But when he felt a tremor go through her body, he pulled her close and roughly turned her toward him.

"I've missed this," she said softly, a catch in her voice.

"Me, too," he said. His hands gripped her shoulders. His heart accelerated. His eyes searched the depths of her hazel eyes. So she'd missed him, after all.

"I mean the stars," she said with a slight tremor in her voice.

"What, they don't have stars in Chicago?" he asked dryly, dropping his arms to his sides.

"Not like here. Not in the city." The wind picked up and rustled the leaves in the willow trees; somewhere, a faraway owl hooted in the distance. She sighed as the moon came out from behind a cloud. "It's beautiful."

"So are you," he muttered. Then he wished he hadn't. She stiffened as if he'd insulted her. And a wary look came over her face. As if she couldn't trust him. Or herself. He reminded himself she hadn't missed *him*. She'd missed the view of the constellations. She'd never once said she was glad to be back. Or happy to see him.

But she *was* beautiful with moonlight in her hair and the starlight in her eyes. So beautiful, it hurt to look at her. It hurt him to think of what they'd missed these past six years. How little they knew each other anymore. But it didn't hurt her. She was looking up at the sky with a dreamy half smile on her face, probably thinking about the man in the moon. But not him.

"That's the first nice thing you've said about this place since you've been back," he noted with a trace of bitterness. "That the sky is beautiful here."

She drew her eyebrows together. "Really?"

"Really." He looked over her shoulder at the Bronco. He couldn't stand in the driveway all night, wishing for the impossible, that Margaret gave a damn about him except as a way to increase circulation for the magazine. "Now, where's my mail?"

She led the way to the car and opened the back doors to reveal three huge regulation U.S. mail sacks bulging with letters.

"Holy Toledo!"

"That's what I said," she said.

"What am I gonna do with it?"

"Read it, answer it."

"I'll need help."

"Maybe we can go through them, sort them out."

"Now?"

"Well...are you busy?"

He shrugged and grabbed a sack from the back of her car. She followed him into his living room. He went back for the other two sacks. When he returned, she was studying the room with a critical eye.

"Don't get any ideas about redoing my parlor," he warned.

"How did you know?" she asked with a smile that tilted the corners of her mouth and brought a sparkle to her eyes. If only she'd look at him that way. But what excited her was not him, but his house. If she was beautiful by moonlight, she was more gorgeous by lamplight, especially when she smiled. He swallowed a groan. Stifled the urge to haul her in to the bedroom. He'd get her in there, but he'd have to be more subtle.

"I see that look in your eye. I've seen it before. You can't start in on my living room until you've finished the bedroom." He braced his hand against the fireplace mantel, watched her and waited.

"I suppose not." Absently she ran her hand through her hair and looked at the mailbags for a long moment. "Shall we get started?"

"Sure," he said. *Nice try, Ralston,* he thought as he dumped the contents of one bag in the middle of the floor. "I gotta hand it to you Margaret. You don't waste an opportunity. Using my poker friends to drum up business!"

Margaret crossed her arms over her chest. "Wait a minute. You told me I should stay here and help lonesome cowboys find happiness, instead of decorating houses in Chicago. So that's what I was doing."

"Speaking of decorating, you haven't seen the skylight yet."

"You haven't seen your mail yet." She looked at the pile on the floor. "Don't you want to read it?"

"There's too much," he protested. "I can't."

Margaret noticed the huge stone fireplace was cold and empty tonight. The fireplace that blazed cheerful fires in the winter. Where they'd lie on the bearskin rug, gaze into the flames and make plans. Wonderful plans for the future. The future that never came. She shouldn't have come here tonight. She should have had him pick up the mail. This house was too full of memories. Like the empty walls where her pictures once hung. But it was too late to back out now. She sat down cross-legged on the floor with her back to the fireplace.

"I'll tell you what Aunt Maud used to tell people," she said. "Divide the letters into three stacks. One for definite possibilities. The second for maybes and the third definite no's. Although nobody ever had this much to deal with."

"Not even the sensitive guy with the heart of gold?"

"Not even him."

Cody sat on the worn carpet opposite Margaret, with a morose expression on his face, staring at the stacks of letters between them.

"You ought to feel good about this," she said, flashing

him a brief look. "Knowing you're such a desirable commodity."

"Oh, I do," he said sarcastically. "You're the one who ought to feel good about it," he countered. "You wrote the ad, you arranged the picture. Told me what to wear, what *not* to wear."

"If you bring up your underwear again, or your lack of it, I'll...I'll..."

"What, see for yourself?" he taunted.

"And if you mention that skylight again..."

"You'll definitely see for yourself, won't you?" he asked with a knowing grin.

Instead of answering, Margaret ripped open the first letter, scanned it and tossed it to one side.

"What was wrong with her?" Cody asked.

"Everything. She couldn't spell or complete a simple sentence."

He picked up the picture that fell out of the envelope. "This is her? Wait a minute. What does spelling have to do with it?"

"Nothing. Nothing at all. If you like her, put her in the maybe pile." Margaret didn't know why she was upset. She was not jealous. Not of some blond, empty-headed bimbo. She was just disappointed in his taste. She opened four more letters in quick succession and tossed them in the no pile without saying anything. With her lips pressed tightly together, she couldn't have spoken if she wanted to. There was a tight knot in her throat. The idea of Cody writing to these women, of him *marrying* one of them, disturbed her more than she wanted to admit. She crumpled an empty envelope in her hand and stared at him as he sat there engrossed in a long, handwritten letter.

After trying in vain to read it upside down from four feet away, she gave up. "Have you given any more thought to actually marrying one of these women?'' she asked, struggling to keep her voice light and casual.

"No. Why?''

"Just that you've been reading that letter for the last five minutes.''

"Listen. You'll get a kick out of this one. 'All I want is to fulfill the wants, needs and desires of the man in my life. I'm a devoted, petite, attractive green-eyed blonde in my thirties. I have a great sense of humor, and from your ad I can tell you do, too.''' Cody flashed Margaret an irritating grin. "That's thanks to you,'' he told her. "Since you wrote the ad.''

Margaret smiled grimly. "My pleasure,'' she said.

"Wait, there's more—besides her great sense of humor. 'I have good values and I'm a good listener. Being from Boston, I'd love to hear more about the great outdoors, the wide open spaces, the big sky.' Guess she doesn't know Montana is big sky country, not Wyoming. She goes on. 'I believe in pampering my man with home-cooked meals and…'''

"That's enough. Just put her in the plus column.'' She wished Cody had never agreed to Aunt Maud's request. Wished she'd never agreed to help him. Wished she'd never come back to Second Chance. Or that she'd never left.

Standing in front of his house tonight, smelling the hay and the wild iris that bloomed along his fence filled her with a deep, painful longing she couldn't shake. Seeing the sharp angles of his face by moonlight brought back so many memories of so many other nights. And made her wish they could start all over. But it was too late. If Cody wanted a woman, someone on a permanent basis, he had more choices than anyone in the history of *Lonesome Cowboy*. And it was her fault. She'd helped him. But she wasn't going to do it anymore.

She pushed the pile of letters to one side and stood up. "I have to be going."

He looked up at her as if he'd been a thousand miles away. Or two thousand, back in Boston where some petite, green-eyed blonde was waiting to hear all about the wide open spaces.

"Already? We haven't even made a dent in my mail."

"I know, but I'm tired."

He jumped to his feet. "You're tired! You haven't had to deal poker hands to a bunch of randy cowboys and listen to their insults. What have you been doing all day? Never mind. Come into the kitchen. I'll make some coffee." He draped his arm over her shoulders in a brotherly gesture. Now that he had all these women throwing themselves at him, he was treating *her* like a sister, an accomplice or a secretary. And she didn't like it.

"You don't really want to hear about my day," she said, embarrassed at how crabby she sounded.

"I do," he insisted, guiding her firmly down the hall toward the kitchen. "I want to hear about your day, your week, your year. I want to hear what you've been doing these past six years."

She *was* tired, but he held her so tightly, she couldn't have left if she'd wanted to. And she really didn't want to at all. She wanted to curl up with Cody in front of a blazing fire, lean against him, feel his sandpaper-rough, day-old beard against her face, feel his lips trail kisses the length of her body, awakening her senses, bringing her to the brink of ecstasy and then over the edge as he'd done the other day. As only he could do. She shivered with anticipation even though she knew it wasn't going to happen. Not tonight. Not ever again.

"Cold?" he asked. "You need some of my cowboy coffee."

"Where you throw the grounds into boiling water?"

"Is there another kind?"

She shook her head and he pushed her gently into the plain pine rocking chair that was once his grandmother Mountcastle's. While he made the coffee, she rocked back and forth, the motion hypnotizing her until she'd forgotten her jealousy, her anger and her regrets. Until she was only aware of Cody moving around the kitchen with cool competence and athletic grace. The faint masculine smell of cigar smoke hung in the air. A stack of cards lay in the middle of the kitchen table. Cody laced her coffee with heavy cream the way she liked it. Then he leaned forward and braced his hands on the arms of the rocker, only a whisper away.

"You okay?" he asked. His face was so close, it blurred. His breath warmed her lips. He ran his knuckles up the side of her cheek, slowly, tenderly. Her pulse quickened. She heard the jungle beat of his heart. She wanted to feel it hammering through his denim shirt. Heaven help her, it was happening all over again. A rising passion spreading through her like the flames from tinder-dry oak. The need to close the gap between them, both emotional and physical. The need to make love to him.

She angled her lips to meet his. But he ignored them. He put the coffee cup in her hands. Then he backed away. Slowly. Deliberately. He took a stool and set his coffee on the counter.

"So," he said, "what have you been doing all this time?"

Seven

"**D**o you really want to know?" she asked.

"I asked you, didn't I?"

His voice was gruff but the look in his eyes gave her reason to hope. Maybe he really did want to know. Maybe if she told him what happened, he might finally understand. Once upon a time Cody had understood her better than anyone. Once upon a time she'd told him everything. He'd been her lover and her best friend, too. A wave of longing swept over her. How much she'd missed him...all these years. Missed the talking, the laughing, the loving...

She took a deep breath and the words she'd been storing up for such a long, long time tumbled out. She told him about Chicago. The things she could never tell Aunt Maud. She told him that after being the best artist who ever went to Mountain View High School, the girl whose paintings hung on the walls of the mayor's office, who designed the cover of the bicentennial yearbook, who was

Harvest Home Queen, niece of the town's most colorful character, *and* Cody's fiancée, she went on to be nobody.

"I thought it would be wonderful to be someplace where nobody knew me. Where I could do something without the whole town knowing about it. And it was, in a way. But it was also lonely." She stared out the window into the darkness of the night, thinking of the noisy city streets, the faceless people. "So lonely."

Cody frowned. "But your aunt said..."

"Oh, I never told her I was homesick. I couldn't let her know. She would have been so disappointed."

"You were homesick?" he asked, unable to keep the surprise out of his voice.

"And scared and worried."

"I didn't know that."

"I couldn't tell you. I couldn't tell anyone. That was the worst part. Not having anyone to talk to." A tear trickled down her cheek. Damn. She hadn't cried then. Why should she cry now?

"Why didn't you come home?" he asked.

She gripped the arms of the rocker. "I couldn't. Not after the way I left." She didn't look at Cody. She couldn't. He knew the way she'd left. "Not until I became a success. Which is taking a little longer than I thought," she added ruefully.

"So I never told Aunt Maud or anyone I fell flat on my face when I got there. What a failure I felt like. I had talent. I always knew that. That's why I had a scholarship. What I didn't know was that other people had more talent. And bigger scholarships. My self-esteem plummeted. I switched from fine arts to decorative arts and from there to interior design. Other people came with portfolios, experience and recommendations. I came with an allowance from my aunt and completely unrealistic expectations. I had to work twice as hard as everyone else just to keep my head above water.''

Cody propped his elbows on the kitchen counter and raised his eyebrows. "But your aunt said you were doing so well. Top of your class. Top of the world."

"I never said that." Getting up from the rocker, Margaret began pacing back and forth from the refrigerator to the back door and back again, passing Cody on her way without looking at him. "I didn't say I was on top, but I didn't say I was at the bottom, either. So she jumped to her own conclusions. She never knew how disappointed I was or how depressed. How much I missed..." She almost said "you." She paused. "Second Chance."

"You had too much pride for that," he said.

"Yes." If anyone knew how much pride she had, it was Cody. If anyone understood why she covered her disappointment and put up an act for her aunt it was Cody. "I couldn't let her down. After all she'd done for me. All the hopes and dreams she had pinned on me. When she came to see me I was finally on my own, in my own place that I'd decorated myself, earning my own money. I think she was pleased."

"Oh, she was pleased all right. When she got back, she talked about you nonstop for weeks. About your apartment, about your brilliant career. About the fabulous party you gave for her. About the beautiful people you knew." The bitterness in his voice was unmistakable.

Margaret leaned against the refrigerator. "The beautiful people were friends from school, struggling out-of-work designers like me who wore jeans and baggy sweaters. The fabulous party was a spaghetti dinner where everyone sat on the floor because I didn't have enough chairs." When she paused, she thought she heard the patter of raindrops on the roof. She sucked in a deep breath. Rain...the skylight...Cody.

She held her breath for a long moment, listening, waiting. When Cody didn't say anything, she rushed on, babbling about something, anything. And trying to listen for the rain at the same time. Maybe it was just her imagination playing tricks on her. Making her think tonight was the night. She gave a little shiver of awareness. She studied his shaggy dark hair across his forehead, the way his intense blue gaze never left her face, drinking in every word she said.

"I asked about you," she continued. "She said you were doing great, the ranch was a big success."

"Yeah? Did she tell you she cosigned a loan for me so I could get back on my feet when anthrax wiped out my herd? Did she tell you the whole crew left one winter, everybody but Jake, when I couldn't make my payroll? Did she tell you she personally ordered one hundred pounds of buffalo steaks and gave them out for Christmas presents last year?"

"No."

"Did she tell you I was going out with every available woman in a two-hundred-mile radius?"

Margaret's heart plummeted. "No."

"Probably thought you wouldn't be interested."

"I...I...thought about you," Margaret confessed. She didn't tell him how often.

"What did you think?" he asked, surveying her through narrowed eyes. "That I was suffering from a broken heart, that I'd never recover from your walking out on me? You didn't think that, did you?" he demanded.

"No, no, of course not. I thought you were probably dating every available woman in a two-hundred-mile radius." She tried to smile, but she couldn't do it. All she wanted to do was throttle every one of those women. She *had* thought about him, she'd worried about him and blamed herself for walking out on him. But now she knew her concern was all wasted. Aunt Maud was right. He hadn't suffered at all. A sharp wind blew in the open window and rattled the dishes in the hutch. She glanced up at Cody.

He got off the stool, crossed the room and stuck his hand out the window. "What do you know, it's raining," he said so casually, she thought maybe—she hoped that maybe—he'd forgotten about the skylight. He slammed the window.

The noise startled her and set every nerve end to throbbing. Thinking of the rain, the skylight, the testing of it. Thinking of what had happened in that room, that bed, before the skylight was installed. She wasn't ready for this...this test. She wasn't sure she could pass it. And if she failed... A flash of lightning lit the sky, followed by a roll of thunder a minute later.

Margaret jumped to her feet, crossed the room and looked out the window at the stormy sky. "I've got to go."

"Not safe to go out in this weather," he said, shaking his head. "Besides, we had a deal, remember?" Remember? If she'd forgotten, the look he gave her reminded her. His gaze was a sensual reminder of unfinished business between them.

His hooded, sexy eyes traveled the length of her body, a visual caress that left her tingling with awareness. She remembered his lips taking the same route, teasing, arousing her until she called his name as she arched and came to a climax. She licked her dry lips. And swallowed hard. He was looking at her now, as if he knew that she was reliving the day of his party. As if she wanted to repeat it. Which she most certainly did not.

"What deal?" she said. "All I know is that I promised you the skylight wouldn't leak."

"And if it does?"

"I'll replace it." She told herself to go. To turn on her heel and leave the room. To walk out into the rain and get into her car. She wouldn't melt. She wasn't made of sugar. She was made of sterner stuff. He wouldn't make her stay. He couldn't. And yet she stood there, gazing fascinated into his eyes, getting lost in those dark blue dangerous eyes. So lost, she might not be able to find her way home. Not tonight.

"We'll have a look, won't we?" he asked, taking her hand.

She didn't have to follow him down the hall to the bedroom. She could have jerked out of his grasp and run out the front door. But what kind of decorator would let the client determine whether the job was done properly? She wanted to see for herself. And then she'd leave. Sure she would. What she really wanted was to see for herself what it was like to make love to Cody under a skylight. The very idea was so risky, her heart pounded with alarm.

Talking about the early days in Chicago had made her feel vulnerable. Afraid to go back there. Afraid of the pain, the loneliness. She reminded herself that she had friends now and jobs that came her way, and if she didn't go back, the whole struggle would have been for nothing. Her goal was to keep the magazine going for a year, to sell it and then let her aunt's estate go to the wildlife foundation. No way was she going to spend this year "making a concerted effort to find a husband." Aunt Maud would understand. She of all people.

"Look," he said, switching on the bedside lamp and glancing at the domed skylight. "Not a drop of rain coming in. What do you think?"

She stood in the doorway, looking at him instead of the ceiling. *I think I still love you.* Startled, she looked up. Had she spoken the words, or only thought them? "I think it looks great. Do you like it?"

"I like it," he said. "So far." There was no mistaking what he meant by "so far."

"Have you tried it out?"

"I've tried it out by sleeping under it. Alone." He didn't mention he couldn't work up any interest in other women since she'd returned. He would never admit how much he'd missed her all those years. How much he'd thought about her. Even while he had brief affairs with other women. He couldn't tell her how much he wanted her. Then and now. Especially now. Not until she told him. And that would never happen. Not with her pride. Maybe he was going about this all wrong. Taking it too seriously. After all, what he wanted was to get Margaret out of his system. Relieve the ache inside, any way he could.

"So what about it, Margaret? You can't deny you're curious to see if the old magic is still there. If it will be the same after all these years. Even though you didn't miss me...."

"I did miss you."

The skylight forgotten, he rocked back on his heels. "You did?"

"We were so close back then, I felt like I'd lost my best friend. I had."

"That's all you want, then—your best friend back?"

"Yes. No. I don't know what I want."

"I do." He crossed the room and in seconds he'd lifted her into his arms. She wrapped her arms around his neck and slanted her lips so they could kiss. The kiss brought back memories so familiar, he ached for the past. Except now the kiss was deeper, more urgent than any they'd ever shared before.

On the way to his bed with Margaret in his arms, Cody tripped on the throw rug and they lurched toward the bed and landed with a whoosh on his down comforter.

"Sorry," he muttered, rolling over so she was lying on top of him.

She propped herself on her elbows so she could look into his eyes. "What do *you* want, Cody?"

"You."

"But just for tonight," she murmured, shifting so her breasts were only a few inches from his mouth.

He groaned. Did they have to have this discussion now when he was hot and frustrated and throbbing with unfulfilled desire?

"Tonight, yes." He reached under her sweater and unhooked her bra with practiced ease. The harsh, out-of-control pounding of his heart blended with the pounding of the rain on the skylight. He'd planned this night, thought about it, imagined it. The purpose was to get her out of his system. The object was revenge. He didn't lie to her. He told her it was just for tonight. She told him the same thing. That was all either of them wanted or needed.

After that, he stopped thinking about anything but how she felt in his arms. How much he wanted to sink deep inside her and claim her once again. Margaret slid her sweater off over her head and he buried his face between her breasts, losing himself in the lush contours, nibbling, sucking, until each tight bud was as taut and aroused as his masculinity. Lightning streaked across the sky, turning the room into a fire storm. Thunder rolled overhead. Margaret moaned and got to her knees.

She straddled him, and while he watched with heavy-lidded eyes, she unbuttoned his shirt and leaned over, brushing his shoulders with her silky hair and his chest with her bare breasts. Images came racing through his brain of the past, and his fantasies, and now this. The present. Reality. Where everything blended together into one erotic whole.

He kicked off his jeans and through a haze he heard her gasp at the obvious size and strength of his desire. When she sheathed it in her warm hands, his breath caught on a ragged oath. With her hands caressing him so softly, so gently, every muscle in his body tensed. Murmuring something incoherent, she somehow got rid of her own slacks and silk underwear.

Sitting naked in the juncture of his thighs, her breasts full and firm and creamy white, she looked like a goddess. A goddess come to earth to bring him pleasure. To drive him insane with lust. He felt his control slipping away. He grabbed her by the arms. Held her prisoner with his thighs.

"Not yet," she whispered, and bent over to take him in her mouth.

He shuddered. She was warm and wet and tight and her lips caressed him until a shudder sped through his body. He needed her, wanted her, desired her. Now. What did she mean, "Not yet"? He felt her hands on his face, tangle in his hair. And all the while she kept him in her mouth. Her tongue bewitched him, set him on fire. Until he was desperate for release.

"Now," he insisted in a voice so jagged, he hardly recognized it.

Margaret let him go, tilted her hips forward and he thrust inside her. Barely in control, she rode him, faster, harder, wilder, than she ever had. She feared the fire inside her might consume her completely.

He drove deeper and deeper. He filled her, he made her whole, he made her his. Her flesh burned, her thighs quivered and every nerve in her body was concentrated on their union. Where they joined together. She could no longer think coherently. All she wanted was to give him as much pleasure as he gave her. To show him how much she cared. How much she loved him. It was her last thought before they were swept together into oblivion. She spiraled into ecstasy and called his name. As his control disappeared, he shouted her name. And the thunder drowned out their voices.

They lay together face-to-face on the comforter, welded together as if they'd never come apart. When her heart stopped pounding, Margaret stole a look at Cody's face. His eyes were closed, but the smile on his face made him look like a triumphant warrior. She traced the outline of his mouth as if she could capture his smile. He kissed her fingertips and she sighed deeply.

Her heart was filled with love and a longing to make this moment last forever. Somewhere deep down inside her, she knew it wouldn't, but she was filled with a crazy kind of joy she'd never known before. And Cody was the reason. The first time they'd made love she'd been a mixed-up nineteen-year-old without a clue. The second time, only three weeks ago, she'd taken and given nothing in return. Tonight she'd given as much as she got. It was a soul-shattering experience. For her. But what about him? Did he still hate her? He didn't act like it.

She stared at him, willing him to open his eyes, to tell her he still loved her as she loved him. But he hadn't moved since he pressed her fingertips to his lips. As she watched, a drop of water hit him on the forehead. Horrified, her jaw dropped. His eyes flew open. He jerked out of her arms and sat up straight.

"Hot damn, was that what I think it was?"

A sudden chill filled the room. Margaret wrapped the comforter around her and climbed off the bed. Trembling on the inside, but calm and professional on the outside, she looked up at the skylight.

"I think I know what happened."

"So do I. It was the storm of the century. Thunder and lightning. I'm surprised there's a roof left at all." He rolled off the bed and stood next to it in his full naked glory. Margaret could no longer look at the skylight. In her life-drawing classes she'd seen some beautiful bodies. But his was the most beautiful of all. Long limbs, powerful muscles. Oh, Lord, no wonder she couldn't forget him.

"Come back here," he ordered, opening his arms.

She went. Let the comforter drop to the floor. Threw her arms around him, let the crisp hair on his chest tickle and tease her sensitive breasts, creating havoc in her nervous system. He kissed her. Deeply, profoundly. She kissed him back. Their tongues locked in an erotic dance. She couldn't get enough of him. It scared her to think she never would. They slid to the floor, wrapped in the comforter and each other and made love again on the carpet. And finally, when dawn crept over the mountains in the east, they slept.

Or rather Margaret slept. Her head on Cody's shoulder, his arm wrapped around her, his palm cradling her breast. He was too uncomfortable to sleep. Not physically uncomfortable. Hell, he'd slept on the hard ground in the middle of a snowstorm, keeping his cattle alive. It was his conscience that kept him awake. That and a dull ache in the middle of his forehead brought about by knowing he was going to break it off in the morning. His fever for Margaret cooled slowly as he lay there. Very slowly. Maybe he'd overdone it, trying to exorcise her from his life in one night. But he'd had no choice.

"Margaret," he'd say in the morning, "let's face it, we don't belong together. You know it, I know it. Hell, the whole town knows it. You're here because of the magazine. I'm here because I belong here. You're going to leave. I'm going to stay." He smiled grimly to himself. How could she refute that? She couldn't.

She might say, "But what about last night?"

"Last night?" he'd say. "That was lust and sex. Nothing more." Nothing more than a fire storm, an earthquake and a volcano all rolled into one. His body tightened and grew hard just remembering. Which just proved that she could turn him on, that's all. Even while she slept, her hair brushed his face, her scent clung to him. Which reminded him of the first time they'd made love in this room, six years ago, the day before she walked out on him.

The pain of her betrayal was not as sharp and fresh as it had been six years ago. Before tonight he'd had no idea that she'd suffered for one moment once she rode out of town. He hadn't known she'd missed him. It didn't make any difference, he told himself. She'd missed him because she had no other friends. To damp down any compassion he felt for her, he forced himself to recall her face in the window of the bus, to remember how the rain dripped off his hat as she rode out of his life. She would never ride or walk out on him again, he vowed, because tomorrow or rather, today, *he* was walking out on *her*.

For some reason, the satisfaction he'd imagined feeling wasn't there. It must be the cramp in his leg, his almost constant state of arousal and a numbness in the vicinity of his heart. He slid out from under the comforter, gently cushioned her head on a pillow and quietly got dressed. Before he left, he paused in the doorway and took one last look at her. At her face half-hidden in shadows, the curve of her lips, the arch of her eyebrows. He wondered if she ever dreamed of him the way he dreamed of her. He shook his head. Probably not.

In the kitchen he made another pot of cowboy coffee while his stomach growled. If he'd gotten married there'd be biscuits in the oven, a rasher of bacon frying on the stove and a pile of hash browns in the pan. There'd be a wife who shared his dreams. A couple of kids around the breakfast table. If it weren't for Margaret haunting his dreams, he would have married someone else. God knows he'd had opportunities. He still had opportunities. Three mailbags full of opportunities.

"Mornin'," Jake said, as he walked into the kitchen, his hair standing on end, his eyes at half-mast. "How'd it go last night?"

Cody stared at him for a long moment while the heat rose up the back of his neck. Maybe the storm hadn't drowned out their cries.

"The game," Jake prompted. "Didja come out ahead?"

"Oh...the game. Yeah...no. I don't remember. We quit early."

"Then how come you look so beat?"

While the question hung in the air, Margaret walked into the room as if on cue, her hair a tangle of dark curls, her cheeks flushed, her shirt and pants wrinkled.

"No further questions," Jake said to Cody under his breath.

"Hi," Margaret said, her gaze traveling from Cody to Jake and back again.

"The skylight leaks," Cody explained, averting his gaze from Margaret. "That's why Margaret's here. She's gonna fix it, aren't you?"

"Of course. That's why I'm here." He watched her carefully. There was no sign of lingering desire or tenderness. He listened to her voice. It was steady as a barometer this morning. If he hadn't been there, he wouldn't have believed she'd made love to him with total abandon the night before. Not once but twice. Nor would he have believed that she'd been intimately cushioned against him on the floor only a half hour ago. Her firm bottom wedged against his masculinity. But then she'd been asleep, oblivious to his discomfort, his continuous lust. He told himself she was as cool as a Wyoming winter because it meant nothing to her. Nothing but a chance to satisfy her curiosity. To see if she still had any power over him. Maybe she was just as anxious as he was to end their affair, if that's what you called it. If she was, there was no reason to prolong the moment of truth.

"Actually it's not a leak," she said.

"You could have fooled me," Cody said, pouring himself a cup of coffee. "Looked like a leak, felt like a leak."

"It was condensation. Caused by the difference in temperature. It was warm in your room and..."

"Warm? It was so hot in there, I was burning up," he interjected. Her cool demeanor was getting on his nerves. He was rewarded by seeing a flush spread up her neck into her face. So she wasn't as cool as she pretended.

"As I was saying," she continued with a pointed look in his direction, "the condensation is caused by the difference in temperature between the outside and the inside. If you'd ordered a flat skylight instead of a curved one, that wouldn't have happened."

"*Now* you tell me," Cody said. "Oh, well, I like sleeping on the floor." He slanted a knowing look at her. He wished Jake would leave so he could speak to Margaret alone. And not about condensation. Because if he didn't do it now, he might not be able to do it at all. But his foreman just stood there, drinking his coffee, apparently enjoying having a beautiful woman in the house. Hearing their banter.

"What's all that mail in the living room?" Jake asked.

"Those are all the women who want to marry me," Cody said.

"Holy Jehosephat!"

"That's what I said."

"How ya gonna choose one?"

"Margaret's gonna help me."

"She know what you like?" Jake asked with a glance at Margaret who was leaning against the hutch, her arms crossed over her waist.

"She knows," Cody answered, which drew another blush from Margaret.

"Wonder if I got any answers to my ad," Jake said.

Before Margaret could answer, Cody said, "You can have half of mine. Just pick out somebody who sounds good."

"Ain't that bait and switch?" Jake asked Margaret.

She drew her eyebrows together. "I'm not sure. I wish we could ask Aunt Maud...." There was a long, respectful silence.

"She'd say go ahead," Cody insisted. "There are plenty of women to go around."

"But you're the one who posed..."

"Yeah, yeah. Anyway, help yourself." Cody gave Jake a look that meant kindly get out of here and leave us alone, and finally the older man ambled out of the kitchen and down the hall to the living room.

"Margaret," Cody said urgently, crossing the room and gripping her by the arms, "we have to talk."

"I know. I'm sorry about the leak—I mean the condensation. I'm going to have the carpenter—"

He tightened his grip. "The hell with the leak, the hell with the carpenter. I want to talk about us."

"There is no us, Cody."

"There isn't. That's what I want to talk about. This town isn't big enough for both of us."

"It seemed big enough last night," she murmured numbly. She felt as if she'd had the breath squeezed out of her by a six-foot boa constrictor. But Babou was safely in his cage. She stared at Cody, still reeling from the shock of his words. What had happened between last night and this morning to make him lash out at her like that?

What did he expect her to do now? Pick up and leave because "the town wasn't big enough for both of us"?

"Seemed big enough," he repeated, fighting the urge to lick her lips with the tip of his tongue, to taste the sweetness, to capture her mouth in a slow, deep kiss that would bring her to her knees, literally. Wanting nothing more than to return to that bedroom, despite the damned leak, and make love to her over again.

Did she know what he liked? What a question. She knew how to bring him to the brink of an internal combustion, then pull back and torture him once again with her sweet mouth until he ached, until he throbbed, until he exploded inside her.

"As you know," Margaret said, gathering her wits together, desperately trying to save some small iota of pride left in her, "I'm staying here for a year whether you like it or not. I'm not letting you or anyone else tell me when to leave. If you think the town's too small for both of us, then you leave."

"I can't do that," he said with a frown. He'd planned this revenge for so long, and now that it was here, it wasn't as sweet as he'd imagined. She didn't want to leave. "There's the matter of the letters. I can't sit around all day answering fan mail. I've got breeding, branding..."

"I understand. And I'll be glad to help you sort them out. But right now..."

"Not now." He had to get her out of his house, out of his mind and out of his heart. Get the letters out of his living room. Get her scent out of his clothes, his room and his bed. And he had to take the offensive, do something to shock her, to hurt her as badly as she'd hurt him.

"But soon," he continued. "Because you're right. I need a wife. And *Lonesome Cowboy* is the best way to find one."

Her eyes widened, her lower lip trembled. "What?"

"You heard me. I'm gonna pick one of those gals, maybe the one who wants to hear about the great outdoors and pamper her man with home-cooked meals."

"I see."

"What's wrong? Why are you looking at me that way?" Like he'd knocked her over the head with a horse-shoe.

"I'm just a little surprised, that's all. What about the uh…rich variety of experiences and all that? What happened?"

"What happened? Maybe I've had it with variety. Maybe I'm ready to settle down. It was reading those letters that did it. Made me realize what I'm missing."

Margaret moved her lips but no sound came out. Her mind was in turmoil. Her body was sore and aching from a night on the ground, and her head was pounding. She'd just spent an incredible night with the only man she'd ever loved. After showing him in every possible way that she still loved him, he first suggested she leave town and then announced he was going to marry someone else. Was it something she did, something she said? Whatever it was, it was too late to change his mind. She knew him. She recognized the look in his eyes, the set of his stubborn jaw. Raising her own jaw a notch, she turned and walked out of the room.

"Wait a minute," he said, following her to the front door. "Take the letters with you."

"They're for you," she said over her shoulder. She should never have put Cody in the magazine. She should never have agreed to help him find a wife. Not when he didn't want a wife. Or did he? She was so confused. Her head ached, a lump formed in her throat and tears were only a moment away.

"Yeah, but you said you'd help me answer them. You owe it to me, don't you think?"

Yes, she'd said she'd help him. Yes, maybe she owed it to him, but…she had no idea it would hurt so much. Unable to speak, she nodded and walked faster toward her car.

"I'll put them in the car for you."

She didn't answer. Couldn't answer, not with that lump in her throat. He didn't appear to notice.

"Don't mention it," he said. "And when you get 'em sorted out—what do they call it? In a triage?—then we can get together again." There it was again, that cockeyed grin and sexy leer. As far as he was concerned, this was just another conversation. As far as she was concerned, it was the end.

She couldn't take any more of this. Maybe the town wasn't big enough for both of them. But she wasn't going to leave. He was just going to have to stay out of her way.

"What about Jake?" he asked, standing in his doorway with the sun's rays streaking across the front porch.

"You want me to find him a wife, too, of course," she said as calmly as possible.

He braced his hand against the white pillar and grinned insolently. "That's your job, isn't it?"

She knew what he meant. *It's your job to do whatever I tell you to do. Because you owe it to me. Because you walked out on me.* How long was this going to go on? Making it up to him for what happened six years ago. Margaret wished she could think of some sharp retort, to put him in his place, to wipe the grin off his handsome face. Instead, she turned the key in the ignition and lurched out of his driveway, spinning gravel in her wake. Without looking once in her rearview mirror.

Eight

Margaret drove straight to her aunt's house, and with a burst of strength she didn't know she had, hoisted the bags over her shoulder, one by one, and dumped them in the sun room. Then she closed the door to the room and vowed not to read one single letter, not to even enter the room again, until she felt like it. Which might be never. After she showered and changed her clothes she got back in her car.

She was clean, she was combed and pressed, but she was still angry. Rage and fury surged through her body as she drove to the office. It was Saturday, but she had no intention of staying at home. Not with those letters in the house. The colossal nerve of that egotistical cowboy to ask her to help him find a wife. As if she had nothing better to do. As if that *was* her job. If he hadn't found a wife by now by himself, he must be doing something wrong. That's what she'd tell him the next time she saw him.

As she walked down the raised wooden boardwalk toward the office, she saw two more bags of mail in front of her door and a young woman in well-pressed jeans peering in the window.

"Can I help you?" Margaret asked.

She turned and surveyed Margaret with big blue eyes. "Oh, I didn't hear you coming. I'm looking for one of the men in the magazine." She held up the May issue and Margaret didn't have to ask which man she was looking for. The same one everyone was looking for.

"He's not here," Margaret said politely.

"How do you know which one I'm looking for?" she inquired.

"It doesn't matter. None of them are here." Did this woman really think the men were in the back room just waiting for the women to turn up? "Most of them are out working on their ranches, branding, breeding..."

The woman smiled dreamily. "That is *so* exciting. I wonder if you could give me the address of the man in the centerfold."

"I'm sorry. That's against the rules. The way it works is that you write a letter to the magazine." Margaret glanced down at the mailbags at her feet. "I forward the letters and the men write back if they're interested. I hope you haven't come a long way."

"As a matter of fact I have. I'm on vacation from San Francisco, on my way to Yellowstone with some friends. I picked up the magazine in Cheyenne and I couldn't put it down. Not after I saw *him.*"

"*Him,*" Margaret repeated, frowning at the magazine in the woman's hands. "I see. Well, I'll be glad to give him a letter from you."

"I haven't got a letter. I don't see why you couldn't bend the rules just this once. I just want to meet him, see if he's as sexy as his picture and check out his place. It's not like I'm going to harass him or anything.''

"Of course you're not," Margaret said with a polite smile. "But I have to look out for my clients. They rely on me for confidentiality.''

"Is that all?" the woman asked, giving Margaret a critical look.

"What?"

"Is that all they rely on you for?''

Margaret's cheeks reddened. She took a deep breath. She could not take one more insult, one more innuendo from anybody. "That's all," she said firmly. "Now, if you'll excuse me..." She put her key in the lock, opened the door and kicked the mailbags into the office. Then she deliberately closed the door behind her. She felt like letting loose with a primal scream, but she didn't.

She wanted to open the door and shout to the woman as she drove out of town, "You can have him. You can have his old-fashioned kitchen and his leaky skylight. You can have his old truck and his herd of buffalo. You can take his pride, his obstinence..." But what about his hot kisses, his tender touch, his blue eyes flashing with humor? Could she take those, too?

Margaret stood with her back against the door, breathing hard. Feeling like she'd just run a ten-mile marathon instead of having had a run-in with a reader. Aunt Maud would never have approved. *Every subscriber, every reader is a member of the family,* she'd say. *The family of women, of prospective brides whose wedding pictures will one day join the others on the wall of the office. Don't forget that, Margaret. Every woman deserves to find her soul mate. That's what we're here for. To help her find him.*

"What about me?" Margaret asked sitting in the empty office. "Don't I deserve a soul mate, too?" She waited, but there was no answer. Sometimes Aunt Maud could be maddening.

Margaret's shoulders slumped. Maybe she should have given the blonde his address after all. Maybe Cody would just snap her up and save them both a lot of trouble going through all the letters. She bit her lip and put a lid on the unbecoming jealousy that threatened her well-being.

Margaret worked all morning until it was time for garden club at Beth Hanlock's house at one o'clock. Aunt Maud was the founder and former president of the Second Chance Garden Club and there was no way Margaret could avoid attending. Besides, it was a beautiful sunny spring day and Beth had an Italian garden with a grape arbor built around a fountain with a cupid in the middle gurgling water from its mouth.

"Maud tried to buy that fountain from me," Beth said, putting her arm around Margaret to take her on a tour of the garden, "every time she came out here. She said it was more appropriate for her being in the romance business." She sighed. "Now I feel terrible that I didn't sell it to her."

Margaret shook her head. "It's a beautiful fountain, but it belongs right here where you have it. Besides, where she is, there are probably fountains and gardens and cupids and..."

"And she probably has those heavenly gardeners transplanting, digging, pruning..." Beth wiped a tear from her eye. "I miss her so much."

"Me, too," Margaret admitted. "Even though I was far away in Chicago, she called me every week. She listened to my problems, gave me advice." Not that she'd stopped advising Margaret just because she was dead!

"She was so proud of you," Beth said. "And so are we."

"She may have exaggerated my accomplishments,"

Margaret said. "According to Cody, she said I was on top of the world."

"I never could figure that out," Beth said.

"How I could be on top of the world?"

"No, dear." Beth squeezed Margaret's shoulders affectionately. "Everyone knew you'd be a big success. I mean you and Cody. What's kept you apart all these years?"

Margaret shook her head. "Pride, I guess, and stubbornness. And the fact that we're not really suited for each other."

"Hogwash."

Margaret giggled. It was either that or burst out crying.

"Cody needs a wife," Beth insisted.

"I know. I'm going to find him one."

"What about you?"

"I don't need a husband. I have my career." She'd said those words so many times, she ought to believe them by now. Instead, they sounded hollow and false in her ears. A glance at Beth told her she didn't believe them, either.

"You can have a husband and a career," Beth insisted. "Many women do it. Marlys the librarian is married and so is Gwen, the church organist. You know, everyone's hoping you'll stay here."

"Not everyone, I'm afraid. Some people have expressed a desire to see me leave," Margaret said primly.

Beth handed her a cup of tea from the table under the arbor and looked at her with concern. "When you hear things like that, you have to consider the source, and the possibility that the person may mean just the opposite. I know that Cody's had plenty of chances to marry over the years, but he never did. Your aunt and I both thought it was because no one could compare to you."

A tiny flame of hope flickered in Margaret's chest. The sun shone on the garden and warmed the stone patio as Beth's words warmed her heart. She inhaled the fragrance of the hyacinth that bloomed around the foot of the fountain. She'd forgotten how breathtakingly lovely spring in the valley could be. How it could thunder and rain one night and be sunny and warm the next day. How you could feel angry and depressed one moment and filled with hope and encouragement the next. The snow-capped mountains stood clear and cold in the distance while the sun's rays slowly melted her ice-cold core of anger and resentment.

The women who were pursuing Cody, the magazine and her struggle to build a life in the city slipped away as she sipped tea from a porcelain cup in this beautiful garden. Life, she told herself, could be just as rich, just as full and satisfying in Wyoming as anywhere else. Maybe she should stay here. Run the magazine and decorate houses in her spare time. In the bosom of people she'd known all her life. People who cared about her, whom she cared about.

Beth passed around little sandwiches, and the ladies sat in wrought-iron chairs on Beth's patio to discuss bulbs, mulch and Cody Ralston. Had they been talking about him for the past six years? Did they talk about him when she wasn't there?

"Call me a hopeless romantic," Penny Bartlow said, "but Margaret and Cody are meant for each other. Why else has he been waiting all these years?"

"Maybe nobody else would marry him," Margaret suggested, feeling the need to squelch this constant speculation about her and Cody. "Maybe he's got skeletons in his closet," she suggested.

The women laughed merrily.

"You should have looked," Penny suggested, "when you were at his house last night."

Margaret blushed. They couldn't *know* she'd spent the night, could they? Unless Jake...or Cody... All of a sudden she remembered *why* she couldn't live in Second Chance. Everybody knew everything about everybody else. Forget spring when the earth burst with new life, forget the flowers, the old friends. Forget running the magazine and decorating houses on the weekends. She just couldn't adjust to life in a small town again.

Just then Beth's daughter Jody came out to tell Margaret she had a phone call. The laughter started again and the teasing. They all knew who it was. Margaret knew, too. Who else would track her down like this?

"Yes?" she said into the wall phone in Beth's kitchen.

"Did you send some woman to my house?" Cody demanded.

"No, I didn't. It's strictly against the rules." She could picture him fuming on the other end of the line, his forehead creased, his eyes narrowed to slits in his rugged bronzed face. "Was she a tall blonde?"

"I don't know. I didn't see her. Jake did. Asked her in for some ice tea. He liked her."

"She's too young for him," Margaret said. "I'm sure we can do better than that."

"You'd better do better and you'd better do it fast. He's getting desperate."

"He hasn't gotten any answers to his ad," she explained.

"Use mine. There are plenty to go around."

She frowned. "I don't know if it's ethical."

"Is it ethical that a man is deserted by a woman who'd promised to love, honor and obey, and is left alone in his old age? Why am I asking you? You're the expert on desertion. Are you going to help him or not?"

"Of course I'll help him. But right now I'm at garden club at the Hanlocks'."

"I know where you are. I just tracked you down by calling everyone in town."

"Oh, yes, that's life in Second Chance."

"It's friendly and safe," he said. "What's wrong with that?" he demanded.

"It's friendly and safe and small and claustrophobic. And all anyone wants to talk about here is one thing."

"What's that? Pruning, ground cover, fertilizer?"

"Fertilizer, yes," she said, exasperated. "The organic kind."

She heard a chortle on the other end of the line. "You shock me, Margaret. When will you be home? I'll meet you at your house and we'll go through those letters until we find someone."

"For Jake. But what about for you?"

"That can wait. He's sixty. And he's lonely. I'm only thirty-two. And I'm fine." His stubborn insistence made her wonder just how fine he was. In any case, his concern for his friend heartened her.

She stood in Beth's spacious kitchen, gazing at pictures pinned to the refrigerator of kids and parents and horses and dogs. And she was hit by a sharp pang of longing—as piercing as a spading fork—for a house, a kitchen, kids, a husband...

"Fine. Come by, then. Come for dinner if you want." Her voice was so light and casual, no one, especially not Cody, would ever imagine she had a pressing need to show him she could do a home-cooked meal as well as anybody out there. No one would ever guess how her heart rebelled at the idea of finding him a wife. Now Jake was another story. She'd be happy to find someone for him. Which was why she'd invited Cody for dinner. There—it all made sense.

But he didn't say anything. Not yes or no. Would he refuse? Had he hung up?

"Did you just invite me to dinner?" he asked, his voice rough as gravel.

"Yes. Is that so unusual in this friendly, safe little town?"

She could only remember one other time she'd invited him. Once when her aunt was working late, she was cooking spaghetti. Cody had stopped by. She was nervous. She'd had a crush on him for years. She asked him if he wanted to stay for dinner. In the steamy kitchen, he took off his hat. She took off her apron. He kissed her. Heart pumping wildly, she kissed him back, while the sauce thickened and stuck to the pan. For a moment, she relived the excitement, the butterflies in her stomach and the smell of tomato sauce. There was nothing as thrilling as that first kiss. Unless it was their last one, on his bedroom floor last night. She braced her arm against Beth's refrigerator door.

"Are you making spaghetti again?" he asked, instead of answering her question.

She drew in a quick breath. Unreasonably pleased that he remembered. "I'm not sure," she said. "Right now I'm in the middle of a discussion about perennials. You know, the ones that come back every year."

"What do you call the ones who come back every six years?" he asked.

"Gluttons for punishment."

"Has it been that bad?" Cody asked.

"It's been...interesting."

"Is that what you call last night, interesting?" he asked. "Maybe it's time to talk about what happened."

"What happened was we made love and you decided to get married." She couldn't keep the hurt and bitterness out of her voice. "There's nothing else to talk about. And I have to get back to the meeting." She hung up. Before she went back outside she looked at her reflection in the door of the microwave oven. Her face was flushed and her eyes were too bright. She dashed cold water from the sink on her cheeks and rejoined the group just in time for a debate about pesticides versus organic gardening.

Cody put the receiver down. Maybe it did seem strange that after a night like that he could consider marrying someone else. But that was only because he knew he couldn't have Margaret. What did she expect him to do? Ask *her* to marry him? And then stand by while she broke his heart and walked out on him again?

He looked around the kitchen. If he wanted to find a wife, he had to do something about this room. Margaret was right. The kitchen needed work. Jake had reported that the woman who came to meet him had wrinkled her nose at the cracked linoleum and the peeling wallpaper. Margaret wanted to get her hands on the hutch. Why not let her get her hands on the whole room?

When he thought about her lovely, artistic hands, he thought about last night. The image of her hair tumbling over her shoulders, her beautiful breasts within reach of his lips made his heart pound and his jeans grow uncomfortably tight. Working his jaw into a locked position, he stomped out of the house toward the corral.

What did it mean, her asking him to dinner? Nothing. And he was a damned fool if he thought otherwise. Jake was, too. His bushy eyebrows rose in surprise when Cody told him.

"Tryin' to impress you," Jake remarked, throwing a saddle over the Appaloosa he was breaking in.

"Think so?" Cody asked, narrowing his eyes against the bright sunlight. "I don't think so." The worst thing he could do was to get his hopes up about Margaret. To let down his guard. She almost got through to him last night, almost made him believe she still loved him. Even if she did, what difference did it make? In the end she'd leave anyway.

"Depends on what she makes," Jake said. "If it's fried chicken and biscuits..."

"It won't be biscuits," Cody said flatly. "Margaret's got this thing about my wanting my wife at home, barefoot and pregnant with her hands up to here in biscuit dough."

"When all you really want is?"

"Margaret," Cody muttered. "Damn it to hell and back."

Jake gave him a look so full of sympathy and understanding, Cody turned on his heel and went back to the house. He didn't want sympathy. He didn't want understanding. He only wanted what he'd always wanted—a wife and kids. Loyalty, devotion. If it took a remodeled kitchen to get him what he wanted, he'd do it. First he'd get the wife for Jake, then he'd work on one for himself.

"The reason I'm here," he told Margaret that evening when he walked in her front door promptly at six o'clock, "is to find a wife for Jake."

"Yes, I know," she said, wiping the flour off her hands onto her apron. "And I'm sorry I ever doubted you had a friend. I never really knew him before, but he's a sweet guy. We shouldn't have any trouble finding him a wife."

If he wasn't mistaken, that white apron with the ruffles outlining the fullness of her breasts was the same one she'd worn the last time he came to dinner here. So long ago. The night he'd kissed her for the first time. When the lights were low, their passion flared and threatened to burn the old Victorian to the ground. If it hadn't been for the sauce burning first.

"What about me?" he asked.

"You?" she said. "You saw the mail. All you have to do is narrow it down and write back to the ones you're interested in."

Her voice was so calm and disinterested, Cody realized he'd been wrong to imagine Margaret was hurt or jealous because he'd changed his mind about getting married.

"Did you have time to look through the letters?" he asked, following her into the kitchen.

"No, I haven't. I've been busy." She waved her arm in the direction of the stove where delicious aromas came from steaming pots and pans and from the oven itself.

"Smells good," he said, his mouth watering. "What is it?"

"Chicken with a port mushroom sauce, mashed potatoes with leeks and sour cream, asparagus..."

"Hold it," he said rocking back on his heels. "Where did all that come from?"

"I made it," she said, turning her back to the stove. "Beth gave me the leeks and asparagus from her garden. Then I stopped by the meat market on my way home to pick up the chicken. The port's from Aunt Maud's cellar, and the mushrooms..."

"Never mind. I get the idea."

"You thought all I could make was spaghetti."

"I thought all you could *burn* was spaghetti," he teased while the memories came flooding back. No matter that she wasn't making spaghetti. Forget the years that had gone by. He was once again a shy cowboy, suddenly invited to dinner by the prettiest girl in town. The girl who drew and painted, who won every honor ever handed out, who was destined to "go on" and do big things. When he kissed her, his world turned upside down. When she kissed him back, he knew he had to have her.

Why hadn't he realized then that he couldn't hold her? Why did he think she'd stay in Second Chance when the world was waiting for her? Pride. Ego. An abundance of both. And if he had it to do over again? He'd take her apron and toss it aside. He'd lean forward until his lips touched hers. Watch the sparks fly. Feel his heart pound. Watch her eyes gleam with awareness. No, he wouldn't change a thing. Even if he'd known what lay ahead.

She handed him a glass of deep red wine, jerking him out of his reverie.

"Courtesy of Aunt Maud," she said.

"To us," he said, daring her to say, "There is no us."

She touched her glass to his. She didn't say, "There is no us." She didn't say anything.

Their eyes met, locked and held. Time stood still. Six years of hurt and loneliness miraculously faded away and left the slate clean. Left him free to love again. Cody felt as if a ten-pound weight had been lifted from his shoulders. His mouth quirked in a crooked smile. She smiled back, her lips the color of the wine. Her eyes darkened to brown velvet.

"I missed you, Margaret," he said, his voice husky with emotion. He reached behind her to untie her apron. Her eyes widened. With her tongue she moistened her lips. His hands skimmed the front of her shirt as he removed the apron, brushing against her nipples and causing an instant reaction. She gasped. He felt the blood pound in his temples. "When you left I thought I might die. Can you believe that?"

Margaret staggered backward. Cody admitting he'd been hurt? This tough, macho cowboy was turning vulnerable? Incredible. Tears sprang to her eyes. And love filled her heart.

"I'm sorry," she blurted. "I'm really sorry for what I did. I swear I'll make it up to you. I'm going to find you someone to marry." *It won't be me. You don't want me.*

Someone to marry! He didn't want someone to marry. He wanted to marry Margaret. But she didn't want to marry him. She never had. "Good. Fine." He faked a smile. He ate her dinner. Told her it was great. It was.

They got up from the table, took their coffee and went to the sun room. As they'd done at his house, they dumped the contents of the mailbags on the floor and sat on the rug with the letters in front of them.

"Here's one for you," Margaret said, setting her cup down. "She says, 'I'm a tigress with a cub looking for a tiger like you.' What do you think?" she asked.

Impulsively Cody leaned over and growled into Margaret's ear.

"Is that a yes?" she asked with a shiver of delicious anticipation.

"I don't think so."

"Why, you don't want children?"

"I want children," he said, brushing his hand over her silky hair and tucking a wayward strand behind her ear. "You know that." He wanted children with Margaret's eyes, her warmth and her smile. He wanted them with a fierce longing that surprised him. But more than that he wanted to protect himself from any more pain. "Forget about me," he said, moving away from her. "We're looking for Jake first."

"Of course." Margaret buried her head in a pile of letters, opening, reading and tossing them aside. All the while aware of Cody's wide capable hands sifting through the letters. Remembering how gentle they could be, how skilfully they could bring her to a climax. She reread the same letter three times. Trying to calm her jittery nerves.

She was aware of his clean blue denim shirt, the scent of his spicy after-shave; just the fact that he'd shaved to come to dinner made her heart race with hope. But the thought of Cody having another woman's children caused a sharp pain in her chest.

"Listen to this," Cody said, holding a letter in his hands. "'Aloha. I'm a young fifty, a loving, athletic and very fit lady who's just moved to the mainland from the islands. I have many interests, but my main interest is you.' Think her main interest could be Jake?''

"Why not?"

"She might not like the winters, or the loneliness." Cody watched Margaret's face for her reaction.

"It could be a problem," she admitted. "If you're not from here originally..."

"What if you are?"

"Then there's always something drawing you back."

Cody held his breath. Was there always something drawing Margaret back? Was it him? He had no reason to think so. Only the way she looked at him, the way she cooked for him and the way she made love to him. There was something there. Too bad it wasn't enough to keep her there.

"I told you how homesick I was," she said. "I told you the whole story. But you haven't said anything about what you've been doing these past years, except for all the women in your life. Or did they keep you too busy for anything else?"

"There weren't *that* many," he said. He didn't say there was no one who could compete with her. "I had time to sell off my cattle and invest in buffalo. Big mistake."

"Why? It's delicious."

"You're in the minority. A big restaurant chain canceled their order."

"That's too bad."

He shrugged. She was sympathetic because she felt sorry for him. He hated that. He ground his teeth together. He should never have told her he'd missed her.

"Here we go," he said, opening another letter. "'I'm a brainy, sexy Scorpio. I like holding hands in the movies and long walks in the rain.' Wonder if she likes making love in the rain.'' He glanced up in time to see Margaret's face turn scarlet.

"The carpenter will be there on Monday to make some drain gutters," she said. "You'll never have to worry about rain again."

"I'm not worried. I enjoyed it." He willed her to look at him, to admit she enjoyed it, too, but she acted like she didn't hear him.

"I hope you haven't forgotten we're looking for someone for Jake," she said, holding a sheet of pale blue stationery in her hands. "'I have seen every Western movie ever made. I dream of living on a ranch with someone who looks like Brad Pitt.' Hmm," she said, "I wonder if she'd take someone who looks more like Clint Eastwood. I would."

"Would you?" Cody asked. "What *are* you looking for? I know, you're not looking—but if you were."

She looked up. "If I were, I'd want somebody with a sensitive soul—maybe a poet or an artist—someone kind and gentle—"

He cut her off. "Good luck."

She tilted her head to one side. "Of course a man doesn't have to be a poet to be sensitive," she said thoughtfully. "He could be anything. A fire fighter or a logger..."

"Or a rancher?"

"A rancher who's rugged on the outside but sensitive on the inside would be pretty hard to resist," she admitted, studying Cody from under lowered lashes. The most irresistible thing about Cody was that he didn't know how attractive he was. However cocky he acted, underneath was a basic modesty, a lack of interest in his looks, an underestimation of his charm. He bragged about his conquests only because she'd hurt him. Because he had something to prove to her. She didn't know why she hadn't seen that before.

He shifted and leaned back against the wicker chair, his long legs straight out in front of him. "Well, I hope you find one," he said.

"I did find one," she murmured. "But I let him go."

There was a long silence. Aunt Maud's grandfather clock chimed in the distance. She stared at the letter in her hands, feeling the heat of his gaze. Feeling the questions hovering in the air. *Why, why why?*

"I was so young," she said. "And I didn't know what to do."

"So you left."

"Maybe I shouldn't have. Maybe I should have stayed," she said, unsettled by the pain she saw in his eyes.

"Then you never would have known if you could make it or not," he said. "You would have always resented me for holding you back."

She crumpled an empty envelope and squeezed it in the palm of her hand. "You think so?"

"I know so."

"But you hated me for leaving."

"I don't anymore. I can't."

She blinked back the tears in her eyes. "That means a lot to me."

Abruptly he stood. "I'd better go."

She raised her eyes, letting her gaze travel up his legs, to his hips, his narrow waist and broad chest. "So soon?"

"Yep. I'll just take those two letters and give them to Jake." He stuffed them in his back pocket. "If you find any more…"

"I'll save them for you."

"Thanks." He held out his hand and pulled her up from the floor. "And thanks for the dinner."

He shook her hand. She expected warmth. At least a kiss. She got a cool handshake. As if she was some casual acquaintance. She felt like a deflated balloon. When she'd said, "Maybe I should have stayed," she thought he'd say, "Yes, you should have." Instead, he turned understanding. Kind. Sympathetic.

Thank God he was leaving. Because her heart was so full of love, it threatened to spill over. Another minute and she would have thrown herself in his arms and told him to stop looking for a wife. Because if he didn't marry her, she might die. And that's when she'd find out what it felt like to be dumped. Oh, he'd be tactful. It was part of the cowboy code. They weren't mean to women or animals. But he'd get the message across one way or another. He didn't hate her, but he didn't love her, either. And what's worse, he didn't trust her.

She walked him to the door, watched the lights of his truck disappear into the night.

In her dreams she called him back. In her dreams he told her it was too late. And in the morning she knew it was true. It was too late for them.

Nine

It was too late for them, but it wasn't too late for Jake or for Cody's kitchen. Both of which kept Margaret busy for the next three weeks as she helped Jake write letters and scraped, sanded and retiled Cody's kitchen. It was a Sunday afternoon; she was polishing Cody's grand-mother's hutch while Jake leaned on the kitchen counter, spun his hat in his hand and watched her.

"Lookin' good, Ms. Margaret," he said, admiring the satin-smooth finish.

She glanced up at the tall foreman in his stiff new jeans, the shirt she'd ironed for him and his string tie. "Looking good yourself, Jake. Are you nervous?"

"Naw. Well, maybe a little. It if works, I'll have you to thank."

"If it doesn't work, there's plenty more where she came from."

"I was wondering…if it wouldn't be too much trouble.

Would you stay to dinner? Then Hannah won't be the only lady. You know what I mean?''

"Oh, oh...of course. I'd be delighted." She stopped rubbing the wood. "But I'm not sure Cody will be...delighted, I mean.''

"'Course he will," Jake insisted. "'Bout time he thanked you for all your hard work.''

"I've enjoyed it." More than that. She'd loved it. Spending evenings and weekends working on these two projects had been a labor of love. She was turning the room into a real country kitchen with limestone tile floors from the nearby quarry and refinished wooden cabinets and counters. She'd ordered strip lights for under the top cabinets, task lights above the sink and had plans for an island work space.

Cody had given her a green light. Said he still had money left over from the fifty thousand dollars Aunt Maud paid him for the centerfold, and had a potential big deal in the works, involving his buffalo.

"Don't know what we ever did without you around here," Jake remarked.

"I'm not finished yet. I won't quit until I see you married and I finish the kitchen.''

"What about Cody? You gotta get him married next, don't you?''

"That won't be any problem," she assured him, rubbing harder than necessary at an imaginary spot. "He doesn't really need my help.''

"Sure?" he asked, his shrewd eyes seeing more than she wanted him to.

"You saw the bags of mail. He just has to find the time to read through the letters and answer them.''

"Wonder if he ever will?''

"Find the time?" Margaret asked.

"Get married.''

"Oh." The image of Cody in his tuxedo standing at the front of the church waiting for a bride that wasn't her made her feel sick. She'd scarcely seen him these past weeks, and not one hostile or bitter remark had crossed his lips. No remarks at all had crossed his lips. When she arrived after work he was in his office. And when she left later in the evening he was still there. He was working on his big deal. Then three days ago he'd left for Cheyenne to sell his buffalo. Making it even easier to avoid her. Said he'd pick up Mrs. Hannah Vanderlay at the airport on his way back.

Running a ranch was a business. Funny how little she'd known about his work before she left Second Chance. Funny how little he'd known about hers. But then she didn't have any work in those days. Just art, and that was only a hobby for her.

"Speak of the devil, where is he?" Jake asked, peering out the kitchen window. "Should be here by now."

When Cody's truck finally pulled into the driveway, she and Jake exchanged nervous glances. Then Jake pressed his face against the window. Margaret removed her old, stained shirt and put her rag and polish away. She rubbed her damp palms against her jeans as she followed Jake to the front door, almost tripping on his heels.

She hung back in the doorway, watching him walk slowly to the truck then shake hands with a tall, nice-looking woman of about fifty. She continued watching until they'd gone off on foot on a tour of the ranch. Then she heaved a huge sigh of relief.

"I think I was as nervous as he was," she said as Cody joined her on the front porch.

Cody raised his eyebrows. "You, nervous?"

"I feel responsible for this."

"You are," he agreed. "Right or wrong."

"Wrong? Was there something wrong with her?"

He shrugged. "She seems fine. God, I hope it works," he said, running his hand through his hair.

"Why shouldn't it?" she asked.

"It's a risky business, getting two people together. People who don't know each other. Even people who do."

She nodded. Who could deny it? "Well, it's up to them now," she said. "Jake asked me to stay to dinner. I think he thought if there was another woman... If you'd rather I didn't..." It was obvious from the look on his face, he had mixed emotions. Why? Only three weeks ago he'd asked her to ask him to dinner. Now he looked at her as if he'd rather have Babou join them.

"Stay for dinner," Cody said. "By all means." Then he turned and went into the house, leaving her on the porch feeling bewildered. Bewildered and stupid.

"Wait a minute," she called, following him through the house.

He turned and she almost ran into him. The tension in the air was palpable. "Yeah?" he asked.

"Are you mad at me?"

"What for?"

"I don't know. For redoing your kitchen. For finding Jake a wife."

"I'm not mad. I'm grateful. I even brought you a present."

"A present?" she repeated. "But..."

"I'll get it." He went back outside to his truck.

She didn't want a present from him. She didn't want any souvenirs to remind her of him after he'd married someone else.

Cody walked out to his truck. He wished he'd never asked Margaret to find Jake a wife or remodel his kitchen. He didn't want her in his house anymore. Her presence was driving him crazy. He'd been hiding from her for the past three weeks and he couldn't hide anymore. He'd pay her off, give her a gift and they'd be even. Almost even. There was only one more thing left to even the score.

He'd been thinking about that every night for the past three weeks. As he listened to her pry off tiles, scrape and pound and paint and varnish, he paced his office like a caged tiger, wanting to join her, to talk to her, tease her, wanting to watch her at work, her face flushed with effort, her eyes bright with the energy she put into the job. But he couldn't trust himself to keep his hands off her. There would be only one more time. One more night. When the time was right.

He took the package out of his car and he knew it had to be tonight. He couldn't wait any longer.

She was waiting on the porch. Wordlessly he handed her the package.

"What is it, a snakeskin wallet?"

"Nope, Babou is still in his terrarium in the bunkhouse. Open it," he instructed.

She tore open the brown paper wrapper and let it fall to the ground. Then she opened the small wooden box in her hands. "Paints," she said, fingering a row of little silver tubes.

"I thought maybe you'd take it up again. You still have the easel."

"But not the talent."

"Would you shut up about the talent? You *were* good. And who cares. You loved painting."

"I know I did. But I thought the only things worth doing were the things worth doing well. Very well."

"That's not true. They're only worth doing if you have a good time while you're doing them. Take breaking horses. I love the thrill of taming a wild horse. But I've been thrown more times than I can count. Jake's the expert. Known all over the county for his way with wild animals. But I keep doing it, loving it. Make sense? I don't know.''

''Yes, it does make sense. Thank you.'' She smiled slowly and his heart lurched in his chest. A dozen other emotions all warred for a place in his heart. Everything but love. Love was out of the question. He'd stopped loving Margaret the day she rode out of town. Not only would he never love Margaret again, he'd never love anybody. Who needed it? Instead of love, there was respect, admiration and, of course, lust.

Right now lust had taken over. Being away from here, away from her, had driven him wild. He'd thought about her every waking minute and dreamed about her every night. After selling his buffalo he'd wandered down the main streets of Cheyenne looking for something to bring her. He wanted to buy jewelry. He pictured her wearing a gold necklace. And nothing else. But jewelry would send the wrong message. Then he passed an art supply store. He thought maybe... Now he wasn't so sure she liked the paints.

''If we want to impress Jake's lady, we'd better shower,'' he said, wiping a smear of dirt off her cheek with his finger.

''We?'' she asked, her eyes widening.

''Yeah, why? Oh, you mean *together*.'' He shook his head in mock horror and let his finger glide down to outline the fullness of her lower lip. ''You amaze me, Margaret.''

''We've never done that,'' she said, her gaze locked on his. Her lip trembled at his touch, her eyes darkened from caramel to chocolate brown. Desire flared between them. Unmistakable. Sizzling hot and lightning bright. She did nothing to hide it. Neither did he. He was sick of hiding. Even sicker of hiding his feelings. He put his hand on her shoulder, hoping to steady the whirl of feelings inside him.

"So much we haven't done," she murmured, one hand holding the paints, the other palm flat against his pounding heart.

"What are we waiting for?" he demanded, propelling her toward the bedroom, his eyes glazed over, his grip tight on her shoulder.

He locked the bedroom door behind them. Kicked off his boots. Tore off his jeans. Saw her do the same. With breathless speed he ripped off his shirt, let it fall to the floor. Then went into the bathroom and turned on the shower. The glass door steamed up. She came to him, wearing only her gold hoop earrings, and his blood roared in his ears.

The water sluiced down on them, stinging hot and invigorating. As if he needed to be invigorated. He picked up the bar of sandalwood soap and its fragrance mingled with hers and filled the air. He ran the soap over her body, turning it slick and satin. Her firm breasts swelled as he lathered them. Her nipples puckered and tightened as his fingers brushed across them.

"Oh, Margaret. You're so beautiful."

"You, too," she whispered, taking the soap from his hands. In long lazy strokes she washed his shoulders, then ran her fingers through the hair on his chest. He sucked in a ragged breath, then her skillful hands moved lower to slide between his legs. His ache grew stronger, impossible to control. He took the soap out of her hand and tossed it in the soap dish, wanting to prolong the ecstasy, the exquisite pleasure of having her body so close, so wet, so responsive.

She was right. There was so much they hadn't done. Washing each other's hair was one of those things. She giggled, then gasped as his hands massaged her temples.

Shampoo ran down between her breasts. She raised her arms and he cupped her bottom and brought her close, closer, lifting her so he could thrust himself deep within her.

When he couldn't wait any longer, he exploded inside her. She buried her head between his neck and shoulder and he felt her hot tears mingle with the hot water against his skin. Wordlessly they clung to each other. The water ran down their faces, their shoulders and their legs. Welded together, they didn't move until the water gradually cooled and Margaret shivered in Cody's arms.

Stepping out of the shower he flipped on the wall heater and wrapped her in an enormous white towel. Then he rubbed her gently, from head to toe, hearing her little cries of delight as he touched each sensitive area. She kissed him—soft butterfly kisses at the corner of his mouth, behind his ears and along his jaw.

He gripped the edges of the towel as he realized what they'd done and what he hadn't done. "This is a hell of a time to think of it, Margaret, I never asked you... We've never used any protection."

"I know. I meant to tell you, I'm on birth control for my painful periods."

"You need a good back massage," he said.

She nodded, a smile curving her lips.

Through the bathroom door came the dull, faraway sound of someone knocking.

"This is what happened the last time I was in this bathroom," she said, gripping the towel tightly across her chest.

"I don't believe it," he muttered, stalking out of the bathroom, still naked. "What is it?" he yelled.

"Cody, that you?" his foreman called.

"Who else would it be?" he asked with a glance over his shoulder at the crack in the bathroom door.

"Gonna take Hannah for a ride."

"Good. Fine."

"Thought you and Margaret might want to come along."

"Not...now," he said, his vocal chords stretched tight.

"Can't find the new saddle."

"I'll be right there," Cody said.

"Sorry."

He couldn't be as sorry as Cody was, to leave Margaret wrapped in a towel in his bathroom. Or as sorry to find her gone when he came back. He swore loudly and went looking for her. But he didn't find her until dinnertime. Then he found her in the bunkhouse kitchen, helping the cook roll out biscuit dough. He did a double-take.

"What's this?" he drawled. "Next thing you know you'll be plucking chickens."

She tossed a floury lump of dough at him. "Don't push your luck, Ralston."

He grinned and joined the crew who were making polite conversation and gazing curiously at Hannah Vanderlay, Jake's lady. At the long dinner table Cody sat across from Margaret. Her hair gleamed silky clean under the brass chandelier, and he knew it wouldn't be long before he could bury his face in her curls, bury himself in the warmth of her body. The body he'd just washed. Washed and worshiped.

But he had an obligation to act like a host for a few hours and not a lovesick cowboy. He could handle it. He could handle anything, knowing that soon he'd have Margaret to himself again and they'd pick up where they left off. Tearing his eyes away from her, he turned to their guest.

"Tell me, Hannah," he said, serving her a bowl of salad, "how do you like Wyoming?"

"It's beautiful," the woman said with warmth and sincerity.

Jake beamed.

Hannah continued to say all the right things. And Jake continued to beam. Talk about lovesick cowboys, Cody thought, smiling to himself.

Hannah asked questions about Wyoming and Jake answered them. Cody caught Margaret's eye and she smiled at him, knowing they had unfinished business to attend to. He could feel the heat from her body clear across the table. He could smell the soap and shampoo. She answered some primitive need deep within him. He knew that, and yet he wouldn't let himself think beyond tonight. He couldn't or he might not be able to go through with it.

He told himself he didn't love her and she didn't love him. He repeated it like a mantra. But it didn't help the longing deep in his soul to make it so. As they exchanged pleasantries over coffee in the living room, the conversation went on and on. He crossed and uncrossed his legs at the ankles. He declined a request to play a duet with Jake on his harmonica. He stood up and poured more coffee. He looked at his watch. He cleared his throat, but nobody got the hint. He watched Margaret and waited for her until he couldn't wait anymore. Finally he stood and stretched elaborately.

"I'm beat," he said. "Has Jake shown you the stables?" he asked Hannah.

She nodded. But she and Jake went outside anyway, and Cody shot Margaret a heated look she couldn't ignore. In silent agreement they walked—almost ran—down the hall to the bedroom.

"You done good," he said as he slowly, carefully lifted her shirt over her head, letting his hands linger on the sensitive spots, the indentation of her throat where her pulse pounded, the underside of her full breasts as he un-hooked her bra, the triangle of curls as he peeled off her jeans and then her silk underwear. "You made everybody feel comfortable."

"Including you?" she breathed, as she pushed him gently against the wall and unbuttoned his shirt. Suddenly the mindless haste of their previous lovemaking was gone. Slowly, carefully she unzipped his jeans and tugged at them until they fell to the floor and he stepped out of them.

His breath grew ragged. "Excluding me. I was getting extremely *uncomfortable.*"

"I noticed you don't wear boxers anymore," she said with a glance at his manhood.

"Is *that* what this is all about? My underwear?" He kissed her on the lips, drawing her lower lip into his mouth.

"You know what it's all about." She looped her hands around his neck, pressing her peaked nipples against his chest, and pulled him toward the bed.

He knew. And he knew how she was going to feel when she found out. Just the way he felt when he realized she was leaving him. But he couldn't stop now. It was all planned. And he wanted her too much. For one last night. He didn't want to think about what happened after that. He didn't want to think about anything. But the words pounded at his subconscious. The last time. The last time.

He operated on instinct. Lifting her onto the bed, he trailed hot kisses up and down her body until she begged for mercy.

"I can't wait anymore, Cody," she moaned. "I want you inside me now."

"I'm coming, darlin'," he promised. "But not just yet."

From her toes, he worked his way up her gorgeous legs

to her knees and then the inside of her thighs, savoring the sweet taste of her skin, loving her response, her quick intake of breath, the little noises she made in the back of her throat. When he reached the sweet hot center of her being, she cried out.

Margaret knew she'd explode if he didn't enter her that minute. She'd begged, she'd pleaded, she'd moaned, she'd cried. If he didn't get the message, she was going over the top without him.

He didn't let her down. He never had. He came into her with one deep thrust that sent her spiraling into ecstasy. And he went with her. They went into oblivion together. The way they were meant to go. Her bones melted. For the second time that day she felt the tears slide down her cheeks.

"What's wrong?" he asked, lying beside her.

She shook her head, her throat too tight to speak.

"Did I hurt you?"

She shook her head again and framed his face with her hands. "I felt like I reached your soul that time. Did you feel it, too?"

He crossed his arms under his head and she pulled away. He didn't feel it. She could tell.

"Never mind. It doesn't matter," she said. But it did. She sat cross-legged on the edge of the bed with the sheet wrapped around her and looked at him. His face was void of all emotion. He didn't feel anything at all. "What's going to happen to us, Cody," she asked, her forehead creased into tiny lines, "when you marry someone else?"

He leaned on his elbow. "I'm not going to marry someone else."

Her heart soared. "You're not?" she asked incredulously.

"I changed my mind. Marriage is not for me."

She gripped the bedpost. "At all? To anyone?"

"Right. Back to playing the field again. Because look what's happened to us. We're in a mess. Tears, misunderstandings and confusion. Not what I'm looking for. And you're not either, right?" He smiled but the smile never reached his eyes.

She started to shake from the inside out. She'd never been so cold. Not even in the great freeze. She felt like she'd just been buried in an avalanche. An avalanche was what it took to open her eyes to the truth. He'd been playing with her all along. While she was stupid enough to think he might marry her when he was really breaking up with her. Talk about confusion. Her stomach churning, she stood, scooped up her clothes and got dressed. With trembling fingers she worked on the snaps of her jeans.

"What about the kitchen?" she asked, avoiding his gaze. "It isn't finished."

"So finish it. You're still my decorator."

"But that's all."

"What do you want to be?" The look in his eyes dared her to say she wanted to be his love, his wife. Then he'd have the ultimate revenge. The pleasure of turning her down flat. He might even laugh while he did it. She wouldn't put it past him.

"Nothing," she said, her head pounding.

"Where're you going?" he asked watching her stalk across the room to the door.

She gripped the doorknob so tightly her knuckles were white. "Home."

"Just like that? So I changed my mind. So sue me. Come on, Margaret. We can still be friends. We can be more than that. As long as we both understand what's going on."

She took a deep breath and sputtered, "What's going on? I thought you and I..."

"You thought you and I..." His mouth fell open in

surprise. "You're the one who said there is no us, aren't you? You're the one who walked out on me. The one who didn't want to be tied down. So why can't you understand that I don't, either?"

"I can. I do. What I don't understand is how you could make love to me like that and then…and then…"

"And then break it off? You don't? You really don't? You of all people." He snorted derisively and stood up to get dressed.

"You never forgave me, did you?" she said, watching him button his jeans.

"What did you expect?" he demanded, jerking his arms into the sleeves of his shirt.

"I expected you to understand. Maybe not then, but now. After all this time."

"Okay, I understand. Are you happy?"

"No, I'm not happy."

"What do you want?" he asked, stuffing his hands into his back pockets.

"What do *you* want?" she asked.

"What I've got."

"It's revenge, isn't it? That's what you want. I can't believe you'd stoop so low."

"Believe it," he said.

Her cheeks stung as if he'd slapped her. She couldn't hurt any more if he had.

"You said you didn't hate me for leaving." she protested.

"I don't hate you. If I did, I'd humiliate you in front of the whole town. I'd walk out on you without any warning."

Margaret put her hands on her hips. "I did not walk out on you without any warning. The night before I left I told you how I felt. You didn't listen. Do I have to spend the rest of my life apologizing for what happened six years ago?''

"No, you have to spend the rest of your life decorating interiors in Chicago. I'm sure you won't want to hang around small, boring, claustrophobic Second Chance.''

"You're damn right I won't. But it's not because it's small and boring, it's because you're in it!'' With that she turned on her heel and stalked out of his room, out of his house and out of his life forever.

They say that anger is better than self-pity for healing wounds, and Margaret's anger was intense and white-hot.

And she fueled it during the next few days with memories of Cody making love to her and then coldly, calculatingly dumping her. She relived every harsh word, every smug remark, every cold glance he'd given her. It gave her the strength to leave again.

As she cleaned out her aunt's desk, emptied trash into a Dumpster, she cleared her mind of all happy memories of Cody. She realized now that for him their lovemaking had only been a physical release. Whereas for her... The telephone rang. She froze. Then exhaled slowly when she heard Beth's voice.

"Margaret, dear, I just heard. Tell me it isn't true.''

"Now, Beth, I never said I was going to stay forever.''

"But I thought—we all thought you and Cody... Was it the skeletons in his closet that did it?''

Margaret choked back a sob. "No. It was just what I said. We're not really suited for each other.''

"You remember what I said. 'Hogwash.'''

"I remember. I'll miss you and the club.''

"Can't you just stay until the next meeting?'' Beth pleaded. "It's at Georgia's. Her honeysuckle should be in bloom by then,''

"It's tempting. Really it is. But I have to get back before I lose all my clients."

"If it's clients you want, there are plenty right here in Second Chance. Just dying to have their interiors decorated. Everybody just thought you were too busy."

"I was. But thanks anyway."

"Cody must be devastated."

"I...don't think so. Just offhand I'd say he's probably relieved."

"Probably? Haven't you told him?" Beth asked.

"Not exactly. But the way news travels around here, I'm sure he knows by now."

Beth sighed. "Are you really going to sell the magazine?"

"Yes, in fact I've had a few offers already." She didn't say they were ridiculously low and not worth considering. She wanted to assure all interested parties, which included the entire population of Second Chance, that her departure was imminent, final and irrevocable. She wanted to squash any rumors that she would be back if only someone would ask her.

"And the house?"

"I've put it in the hands of a Realtor in Cheyenne."

"That's kind of sad."

Margaret nodded, tears filling her eyes as she thought of someone else tending the garden, someone else storing their memories in the attic. "Life goes on," she said bravely, and after promising to come by and say goodbye, she hung up.

On her way out the door with another load of junk, she almost ran into Jake on the raised walkway. She set the trash can down between them. "How are things? How's Hannah?"

His eyes lit up, his smile stretched across his face. "She's pretty wonderful and she's just what you suggested. Independent and strong-minded and looking for a simpler way of life. I just put her on the bus. But she'll be back. To stay.''

''That's wonderful,'' Margaret said. ''You know that day we had our talk in the coffee shop, were you talking about yourself or...or Cody?''

''You mean the lovesick, brokenhearted bull?'' he asked with a grin. ''Guess it could have been either one of us. But I was thinkin' of him.''

''I thought so. Well, I'm glad it worked out so well for you. Congratulations.'' After seven days Jake had found the woman of his dreams. And in six years Margaret had never found anyone to replace the man of her dreams.

There was a long silence while Jake looked through the window at the empty office and the full trash can in Margaret's hands. The creases in his forehead deepened. ''You're...you're leaving?'' he said at last.

''Yes. I came for the funeral. It's over, so I'm going back...home.'' Home. Yes, Chicago was her home now. That's where her job was and her apartment. And most important, that's where Cody wasn't.

Jake's mouth twitched. Margaret wondered if he'd mention Cody. She certainly wouldn't. ''We'll miss you,'' he said.

Margaret wondered who ''we'' was. He and Hannah? The whole town...minus one? ''I'll miss you, too,'' she assured him.

''I had the feeling you were thinking of staying,'' he said slowly, drawing out his words.

''Me? Oh well, at one point I did. I actually thought about taking on the magazine, settling down in Second Chance, but things change. I'm just happy I could help you find yourself a wife, and such a fine one.''

''I'll be forever grateful for that, but...what about Cody?''

She stiffened at the mention of the *C* word. "How is he?" she asked politely.

"He don't look so good to me."

"That makes two of us," she said stiffly. "He doesn't look good to me, either."

He nodded. "He said you thought Second Chance was too small and too something else for you."

She clenched her hands into tight fists. "Claustrophobic. Damn him anyway. I'll bet he's telling everyone in town I said that."

"Don't think he's seen anyone in town. He's been out every day breaking in a new horse."

"Isn't that dangerous?"

"For him, yes. But Cody's stubborn. Once he decides to do something..."

He did it single-mindedly. Like paying her back. All the time he'd flirted with her, eaten with her, kissed her, comforted her, made love to her. All that time he'd been thinking of only one thing—getting even. Her head spun and anger surged through her veins.

"You okay?" Jake asked.

She forced herself to breathe slowly. "I'm fine. I'd better get back to work."

Jake held out his hand. "In case I don't see you before you leave..."

"Goodbye." She shook his hand.

Margaret shook a lot of hands before she left at the end of the week. She didn't realize how many friends she had in Second Chance. When she finally got on the bus for Cheyenne on Friday, the entire bridge club was there to see her off as well as the garden club.

As the bus left Main Street and headed out of town she almost thought she saw the shadow of a tall man. But when she pressed her face against the window, he was gone. It couldn't be him. Although he might want to be sure she was gone, he wouldn't want to give her the satisfaction of seeing him there on the street.

She gripped the metal handrail and let the tears run down her face. There was no one to see her cry. All her friends were back there in Second Chance. And ahead of her...

Ten

From the shadow of a willow tree Cody watched the bus pull out of town. The triumph he'd imagined feeling wasn't there. But neither was the devastation he'd felt the last time this happened. The truth was, he didn't feel anything at all. He was empty of all emotions, and he was numb from head to toe. She was gone. Gone was her smile, her elusive, expensive scent, her city clothes and her liquid amber eyes. Gone, and good riddance!

Their last confrontation echoed in his head. He pounded his fist into his palm so hard, it left an ugly red mark. He *would not* think about her.

He walked down Main Street back to his truck, passing friends without speaking, without seeing them.

"Hey, Cody." Will Dorsey blocked his way with his burly body. "I just heard. Looks like I owe you some money."

Cody stared at him blankly.

Will waved a handful of bills in front of Cody's face. "The bet, remember?"

Cody wanted to take Will by the outstretched hand and throw him over his shoulder along with anyone else who wanted to remind him of the bet, Margaret or just about anything else. "Forget it," he snapped.

"Oh, so now you're a big buffalo rancher, you can afford to forgive your debts. Well, you can't forgive me. I pay my debts. And so do the other guys."

"Fine." Cody tried to walk around Will, but Will stood his ground, like a stubborn bull.

"Helen says Margaret left. That she's shutting down the magazine, selling the house—everything. Says it's because of you. You made her do it."

Cody sucked in an angry breath. "Nobody makes Margaret do anything. Especially me. Nobody made her leave last time and nobody made her leave this time. She left because she wants to."

"Guess she thinks it's pretty dull around here."

"Dull and boring." He left off claustrophobic. It seemed like overkill.

Will raised his eyebrows. "She didn't look bored at your birthday party. Looked like she was having a good time."

"Yeah?" Cody didn't want to think about the birthday party. About her lying on his bed planning the skylight. He couldn't sleep in his bed anymore and look up at the skylight. He couldn't sleep anywhere anymore. He had terminal insomnia. He wandered around the house in the middle of the night trying not to think about Margaret. Trying to forget the smile on her face when she told him she'd reached his soul. Right about now she'd have come to the conclusion he didn't have one.

She should have known he couldn't commit himself

again. Especially to her. Even if he didn't know it himself. She knew him better than anyone.

"Maybe she *was* having a good time," Cody admitted. "But she doesn't belong here. She was gonna leave sooner or later. Might as well be sooner."

"Did you dump her?"

"Honest to God. How do these rumors get started? How can you dump somebody you're not even involved with?" Telling such a blatant lie made the heat rise up the back of his neck.

"You're saying there was nothing between you?" Will asked.

"Nothing but hard feelings." Cody glanced at the sky, wondering if he'd be struck down by lightning for lying. There was more than hard feelings between them. There was trust and mistrust, love and hate and pain and ecstasy. All that and more.

"Then you won't miss her, right?"

Cody had half a mind to wipe the knowing smile off Will's face with his fist, but he restrained himself. "Did I miss her last time she left? No. Will I miss her this time?" He grabbed Will by the collar. "What do you think?"

Will's eyes bulged. "Helen thinks Margaret's still in love with you."

Cody rocked back on his heels and glared at his friend. "How could she still be in love with me when she never loved me in the first place?"

"She was gonna marry you, wasn't she?"

"I don't think so."

"But she got halfway down the aisle."

"Halfway isn't good enough." The vision of Margaret in her wedding dress flashed before his eyes. He thought of that night in the attic. The dress in the trunk. Her saying

I sent it back to Aunt Maud in case... In case she got married to someone else. That's what she meant.

"Gotta go," Cody said, and made a sharp left turn to cross the street. Then he wheeled around. "Selling the house, you say?"

"Yep."

He nodded and strode across the empty street. All he wanted to do was get home before anyone else started in on him. How would he ever forget Margaret if everyone kept talking about her, ad nauseam? Last time Margaret left, people kept their thoughts to themselves, out of respect for his feelings. This time they thought he was to blame for Margaret's leaving. *She doesn't belong here. She doesn't love me.* How many times did he have to say it before people believed it? How many times did he have to say it before *he* believed it?

He tried repeating it night after night, week after week, as he lay on the couch in the living room. Then he tried counting buffalo instead of sheep. But he still couldn't sleep. He didn't know why. He had nothing on his mind. Nothing to worry about. He was on a roll, selling buffalo as fast as he could fatten them up. He should be out celebrating at the saloon, buying drinks for everybody. He could afford it.

He could afford to finish the kitchen, too, but he didn't. Giving in to sleeplessness one night, he tossed his blanket to the floor and staggered into his kitchen to make a sandwich. He looked around in the semidarkness at the new lights still in their boxes and the grout that had hardened and turned to concrete in the bucket.

The temporary bare bulb that hung from the ceiling went on and Cody jumped a foot in the air and spun around. His foreman stood squinting sleepily in the doorway.

"Don't you ever knock?" Cody asked irritably.

"Knock? On the kitchen door? In the middle of the night?"

"Okay, all right. Don't knock." When Cody's heart resumed beating normally, he looked around the room and said, "Wouldn't you think she could have finished the kitchen before she left?"

"Didja' ask her?"

"You don't ask Margaret to do things. You either tell her or she tells you."

"Ya' miss her, don't ya?" Jake asked, filling the kettle with water.

"Like a pain in the butt," Cody assured him.

"You been acting awful strange. Walkin' around like a zombie instead of out celebrating your good fortune."

"You're right. I got plenty to celebrate. Main thing, Margaret's gone."

"Main thing, you settled the score with her." Jake poured hot water over a tea bag into a mug. "Must be a good feeling."

"It is," Cody said a shade too emphatically.

"And Margaret, she got her comeuppance."

Cody leaned against the new counter. "How do you know?"

"I seen her at her office before she left."

"And?"

"And she didn't look so hot. She looked sad and disappointed and…what's that word? Disillusioned. Yeah, that's it."

Cody slammed his palm against the new oak shelving. "Oh, now that you're engaged, you're an expert on women and their feelings. What do you think disillusioned her?"

"I think you did. And I think you did it on purpose. To get your revenge."

Cody stared at him for a long moment. "What is wrong

with everybody around here? Did you forget what happened six years ago? Do you remember how Margaret left me standing like an idiot in the church while she ran away to Chicago?''

"Sure I remember. You won't let me forget. But it's 'bout time you stop living in the past. And get on with your life.''

Cody studied the man's plain, honest face, remembering how Jake had taught him to ride, to rope and to take care of sick animals. How he'd stuck by him all these years, through drought and epidemics of anthrax. Jake had never criticized him the way his friends did for sinking his money into buffalo. He'd been supportive and generous with his time and his advice, which was generally right on.

"And I suppose you've got some advice as to how I should do that?'' Cody asked, planting his hands on his hips.

"Damn straight I do. You get your butt on a plane to Chicago and apologize to that woman. No way did she deserve what you did to her.''

"And then?''

"Then maybe you'll be able to sleep at night. And stop bein' so jumpy. And disagreeable.''

Cody narrowed his eyes. "You think I'm disagreeable?''

"Everybody thinks you're disagreeable. Including the buffalo. Now git out and don't come back 'til you can be civil to your friends.''

"Are you forgetting I'm your boss?''

"Are you forgetting I'm old enough to be your father?''

Cody shook his head and brushed past Jake on his way out of the kitchen. "I've been a real jerk, haven't I?'' he muttered.

The old man slapped him on the back and Cody grimaced in pain. Not from the slap on the back, but from the realization that he'd acted like a fool. And that he'd broken the cowboy code. Cowboys are always polite to women and they never cry. He hadn't cried. Not this time. But he had not been polite to Margaret.

What if she refused to see him, he thought as he threw his clothes into a duffle bag. What if she wouldn't speak to him? What if she hated him? No question about that. She did hate him. With good reason.

Margaret balanced herself on the top of a tall ladder and examined the seal around the domed acrylic skylight. She smiled with satisfaction at the tight fit, secure in the knowledge that even if it rained, the occupants of this decorator showcase home would not get wet. She rubbed her palms together. Her stay in Second Chance had not been totally wasted. She'd learned about weatherproofing. Even better, she'd learned heartbreak-proofing, as well.

In the weeks since she'd left, her anger had faded, replaced by a grim acceptance of her fate. She'd deserted Cody and he'd paid her back. She knew he'd suffered, but she never knew how much until now. She found out how long a sleepless night could be, and how lonely the days that followed. The city was once again a vast empty place filled with faceless people. At least Cody'd had his friends, his ranch, his valley, his town.

The city also had opportunities and she was taking advantage of them. The latest was this decorator's showcase. A chance to showcase her talent. She found she could still lose herself in the job at hand, in the challenge of turning a bedroom into a library, or a library into a bedroom, finding space for a rare book collection, or using a wild West theme with antlers for a hat rack, a faux window painted on the wall with a scene of a wide valley ringed with mountains in the distance and a skylight in the ceiling. Soon throngs of people would come parading through this designer showcase house on Lake Shore Drive, oohing and aahing, taking notes, and hopefully taking note of the bedroom designed by Margaret Kidder.

Margaret took one step down the ladder and froze. She wasn't alone. Someone else was in the room. Come early for a sneak preview.

He was standing in the doorway, hands braced against the molding, legs crossed at the ankles, looking up at her, every bit as insolent as he was that day in her aunt's office. Her face flamed, her hands shook.

She'd imagined seeing him again, but not from the top of a ladder. Not with trembling thighs and muscles made of Jell-O. She'd prefer to be at the controls of a steamroller and smash his sexy, arrogant body flat.

"You! What are you doing here?" she demanded. "How did you find me?"

"Called your office. I'm here to collect," he said, nonchalantly tossing his hat in the direction of the antlers on the wall.

"What?"

"That's right. You owe me. Nobody walks out on Cody Ralston without paying her debts."

Margaret stepped down to the next rung and gripped the sides of the ladder. She was definitely on top of a ladder, but her stomach thought she'd taken a fast elevator ride to the top of the John Hancock Building and left it behind.

"What do you mean?" she asked, trying to keep her voice steady.

He sauntered to the foot of the ladder and tilted his head up. His shaggy hair was longer, his eyes were bluer, his face bronzed by the Wyoming sun. Her heart pounded. Why was he here? What did he want?

"Don't play dumb with me, Margaret Kidder. I've

known you since you were six. I bought you lunch at the diner and you ate my buffalo meat at my party. And all I got out of it was one dinner."

She stared down at him. "You came all this way for one dinner?"

He shrugged. "Thought maybe I could sell some buffalo meat while I'm here, too."

She exhaled slowly. "Oh, it's a business trip."

"Business *and* pleasure." A gleam shone from his eyes as he looked at her. "Speaking of pleasure, are you coming down or should I come up?"

Hurriedly she clambered down the metal rungs before he had a chance to charm his way into her life again. When she slipped on the fourth rung and fell backward, he caught her and swung her into his arms.

"Don't touch me," she ordered, jerking out of his arms as if she'd run into a live wire. And the memories came flooding back. Her first day back in town. Her aunt's office. Cody tossing his hat at the antlers. Cody seething with the anger he'd been storing for six years. All that wasted time. All that wasted energy.

His face clouded over like a Wyoming sky at sunset. "I didn't exactly expect a warm welcome, but I was hoping..."

"Me, too. I was hoping I'd never see you again," she said. "No, that's not true. I was hoping I'd see you locked up in the county jail for...cattle rustling or...or bigamy."

"Bigamy? I can't even get one girl to marry me, let alone two. I can get them to the church, and halfway down the aisle, but that's about it." To Margaret's surprise, he didn't sound bitter. His tone was light. He was laughing at himself. She felt some of the tension ooze out of her neck and her shoulders.

Feeling light-headed and wobbly at this unexpected display of humility, Margaret eased back and sat on the edge of the king-size bed. "Maybe you're not being aggressive enough," she suggested with a catch in her throat. Suggesting Cody be more aggressive was like suggesting his prize bull get a shot of testosterone. "When these women leave you at the altar, maybe you should go after them." Oh, Lord, what was she saying? She was playing with fire here. Did she really want Cody coming after her? Could she ever trust him again if he did?

"That's what Jake said. 'Go after her and apologize.'"

"That's not necessary." As if he thought that's all he had to do.

Restlessly he paced the room. It was unnerving to see him here in this faux-Western room when he was so real, so authentically Western, so authentically sexy. He paused in front of the wall painting, studying the colors and the brush strokes up close.

"You do this?"

"Yes. You recognize the scene, I guess. It's not great, but I had fun doing it. You gave me the paints, remember?" She paused. "And the confidence."

"Uh-huh."

He didn't say what he thought of her artwork or the way she'd done the room. He seemed preoccupied.

"It may not be necessary, but I'm going to apologize anyway," he said.

Margaret stood and smoothed her skirt with damp palms. She straightened the books on the bedside table while her mind spun and her pulse raced. Just like in her dreams Cody had come to apologize. Maybe it *was* necessary. For him. For her. She went to the window and looked out into the busy street without seeing the cars whiz by.

"All right. Go ahead. Get it over with."

He came up behind her. So close, she could smell his leather jacket, his familiar after-shave. Reminding her of the days and nights they'd spent together, of the good times and the bad. A wave of longing and homesickness hit her with the force of a Michigan Avenue double-decker bus. He put his hands on her shoulders and she saw his face reflected in the window. His eyebrows were knotted together, his mouth twisted in a grimace.

"I don't know what to say, Margaret. What I did was unforgivable. Maybe you can find it in your heart to forgive me anyway." His voice dropped and thickened on the last words. Margaret felt the tears spring to her eyes. Cody acting sorry. Cody apologizing. Her knees buckled. If he hadn't been holding her by the shoulders, she might have collapsed and scuffed the refinished oak boards.

"Let's just forget the whole thing," she murmured, and breathed a sigh of relief. She was so tired of feeling hurt and angry and resentful. Now it was over. He could leave. She pressed her palm against her heart to ease the pain that lingered, to still the longing that threatened to overtake her even now. She glanced at his face in the reflection. His expression was unfathomable. And still he didn't leave.

"I'm glad you came," she said at last. "We've known each other too long to stay enemies. Now that you've done what you came to do..." She couldn't say another word over the lump in her throat. She turned and held out her hand. He took it. And pulled her up against his rock-hard chest. The frantic beat of his heart matched her own. Her skin sizzled wherever he touched her. The heat from his body threatened to start a conflagration.

Then he kissed her. Slowly. Deeply. As if they had all the time in the world. As if they had the rest of their lives. He parted her lips with his tongue and she moaned softly. Savoring the taste of him. Knowing she could never get enough of him. Knowing she'd never stopped loving him. And she never would.

With an effort, he pulled back and looked into her eyes. "I came to get you, Margaret. I came to bring you back home." His mouth curved in a half smile while his hand sifted possessively through her hair, setting every nerve end on fire. "Are you coming peacefully, or do I have to throw you over my shoulder and carry you out of here?"

Visitors at the decorator's showcase oohed and aahed over the bedroom with the Western theme. The cowboy hat hanging on the bleached antlers on the wall gave just the right realistic touch. Even better was the sight of an honest-to-God cowboy wearing a leather jacket and an ear-to-ear grin, walking through the house with one of the decorators over his shoulder.

Epilogue

One month later

The church was full. The smell of freesias and lilies of the valley filled the air. Organ music wafted out the open windows. The friendly, worn, weather-beaten faces of the guests turned to watch the bride come down the aisle. She heard the words of her aunt echo in her brain.

I told you he'd wait. He loves you.

You've got your whole lives ahead of you. Both of you.

Margaret's lower lip trembled and she blinked away tears of happiness behind her heirloom veil.

Cody waited at the altar with Jake as best man at his side. His heart tripped a beat as Margaret passed the half-way mark up the aisle. Not that he'd ever let her get away again. He'd wasted six years of his life feeling hurt and angry and he didn't intend to waste another single minute.

He reminded himself that she hadn't wasted any time.

In the six years, she'd grown up, acquired a profession and become a woman. His woman. His heart filled with pride as she came closer. And finally, as the music swelled and he lifted her veil and kissed her, she became his wife.

* * * * *

Available in February 1998

ANN MAJOR

CHILDREN OF DESTINY
When Passion and Fate Intertwine...

SECRET CHILD

Although everyone told Jack West that his wife,
Chantal—the woman who'd betrayed him and sent
him to prison for a crime he didn't commit—had
died, Jack knew she'd merely transformed herself
into supermodel Mischief Jones. But when he
finally captured the woman he'd been hunting,
she denied everything. Who was she really—
an angel or a cunningly brilliant counterfeit?"

"Want it all? Read Ann Major."
—Nora Roberts, *New York Times*
bestselling author

Don't miss this compelling story
available at your favorite retail outlet.
Only from Silhouette books.

Take 4 bestselling love stories FREE

Plus get a FREE surprise gift!

Special Limited-time Offer

Mail to Silhouette Reader Service™

> 3010 Walden Avenue
> P.O. Box 1867
> Buffalo, N.Y. 14240-1867

YES! Please send me 4 free Silhouette Desire® novels and my free surprise gift. Then send me 6 brand-new novels every month, which I will receive months before they appear in bookstores. Bill me at the low price of $2.90 each plus 25¢ delivery and applicable sales tax, if any.* That's the complete price and a savings of over 10% off the cover prices—quite a bargain! I understand that accepting the books and gift places me under no obligation ever to buy any books. I can always return a shipment and cancel at any time. Even if I never buy another book from Silhouette, the 4 free books and the surprise gift are mine to keep forever.

225 BPA A3UU

Name	(PLEASE PRINT)	
Address	Apt. No.	
City	State	Zip

This offer is limited to one order per household and not valid to present Silhouette Desire® subscribers. *Terms and prices are subject to change without notice.
Sales tax applicable in N.Y.

UDES-696   ©1990 Harlequin Enterprises Limited

As seen on TV!
Free Gift Offer

With a Free Gift proof-of-purchase from any Silhouette® book,
you can receive a beautiful cubic zirconia pendant.

This gorgeous marquise-shaped stone is a genuine cubic
zirconia—accented by an 18" gold tone necklace.

(Approximate retail value $19.95)

Send for yours today...
compliments of ▼ *Silhouette*®

To receive your free gift, a cubic zirconia pendant, send us one original proof-of-purchase, photocopies not accepted, from the back of any Silhouette Romance™, Silhouette Desire®, Silhouette Special Edition®, Silhouette Intimate Moments® or Silhouette Yours Truly™ title available at your favorite retail outlet, together with the Free Gift Certificate, plus a check or money order for $1.65 U.S./$2.15 CAN. (do not send cash) to cover postage and handling, payable to Silhouette Free Gift Offer. We will send you the specified gift. Allow 6 to 8 weeks for delivery. Offer good until March 31, 1998, or while quantities last. Offer valid in the U.S. and Canada only.

Free Gift Certificate

Name: _____

Address: _____

City: _____ State/Province: _____ Zip/Postal Code: _____

Mail this certificate, one proof-of-purchase and a check or money order for postage and handling to: SILHOUETTE FREE GIFT OFFER 1998. In the U.S.: 3010 Walden Avenue, P.O. Box 9077, Buffalo, NY 14269-9077. In Canada: P.O. Box 613, Fort Erie, Ontario L2Z 5X3.

FREE GIFT OFFER   084-KFD
ONE PROOF-OF-PURCHASE
To collect your fabulous FREE GIFT, a cubic zirconia pendant, you must include this
original proof-of-purchase for each gift with the properly completed Free Gift Certificate.

084-KFDR2

The Stars of Mithra

Three gems,
three beauties,
three passions...
the adventure of a lifetime

SILHOUETTE·INTIMATE·MOMENTS®
brings you a thrilling new series by
New York Times bestselling author

Nora Roberts

Three mystical blue diamonds place three close
friends in jeopardy...and lead them to romance.

In October
HIDDEN STAR (IM#811)
Bailey James can't remember a thing, but she knows
she's in big trouble. And she desperately needs private
investigator Cade Parris to help her live long enough to
find out just what kind.

In December
CAPTIVE STAR (IM#823)
Cynical bounty hunter Jack Dakota and spitfire
M. J. O'Leary are handcuffed together and on the run
from a pair of hired killers. And Jack wants to know
why—but M.J.'s not talking.

In February
SECRET STAR (IM#835)
Lieutenant Seth Buchanan's murder investigation takes
a strange turn when Grace Fontaine turns up alive. But
as the mystery unfolds, he soon discovers the notorious
heiress is the biggest mystery of all.

Available at your favorite retail outlet.